Dare to Dream. . .

Kin managed to wriggle through the window of Waddy's Taurus and slide down into the driver's seat.

He was in! The thinly padded seat was stiff and unyielding, the well buffered steering wheel thick under his hands. The gearshift knob was in easy reach. Kin grinned, liking the feel of it all.

He took a deep breath, closing his eyes to savor the faint smells of oil, gasoline, rubber, and stale sweat. He could almost see the track melting away in front of him . . . the long back straightaway of Talladega . . . the S-curves of Watkins Glen . . . the high banks of Daytona. He could almost hear the squeal of the tires and the roar of the engines. He could almost feel the air rushing past. . . .

SPEED DEMON

POLE POSITION ADVENTURES NO. 4

T. B. Calhoun

HarperEntertainment
A Division of HarperCollinsPublishers

▲ HarperEntertainment

A Division of HarperCollins*Publishers*
10 East 53rd Street, New York, NY 10022-5299

This is a work of fiction. The characters, incidents, and dialogues
are products of the author's imagination, or if real, are used ficti-
tiously. Any resemblance to actual events or persons, living or
dead, is entirely coincidental.

First printing: February 1999

Cover illustrations by Tony Randazzo
Designed by Jeannette Jacobs

Printed in the United States of America

ISBN 0–06–105964–1

98 99 00 01 02 10 9 8 7 6 5 4 3 2 1

CONTENTS

A SURPRISE VISITOR

Kin Travis couldn't believe his eyes. It was late, the concert was over, and the Sudden Falls High School gymnasium was almost empty. It had been a long day, full of surprises, and Kin had just been thinking how nice it would be to collapse into his bunk in his grandfather's trailer and sleep for about twelve hours straight.

But it seemed there was one more surprise in store today. Someone new had just entered the gym—someone who seemed completely out of place here in rural North Carolina.

Kin's twelve-year-old sister Laura was the first to speak.

"Aunt Adrian! What are you doing here?" Laura exclaimed, sounding just as surprised as Kin felt.

She hurried to the edge of the stage and hopped down, facing the tall, angular woman standing in the middle of the gym floor with her arms folded across the chest of her dark-blue tailored suit.

"Hello, Laura," Aunt Adrian replied in her crisp, Boston-accented voice. She smiled fondly at Laura, Kin, and their seven-year-old brother Larry, better known as "Laptop." "I don't like to complain." Her smile faded as she patted her short salt-and-pepper hair. "But when I sent my dear, departed brother's children down here for the summer, I naturally expected they would be cared for properly. However, if the person who's supposed to be taking care of you can't even manage to return my phone calls . . . "

Kin's grandfather, Hotshoe Hunter, had been standing to one side of the stage talking to his friend, Infield Annie. But now he stepped forward and placed a callused hand on Laura's shoulder. "You referring to me?" he asked Aunt Adrian evenly. She was a formidable-looking woman, especially when she was angry, but Hotshoe didn't look scared. He had been a race car driver in his younger days, and it took a lot to frighten him.

Aunt Adrian turned her laser-beam gray eyes on

Hotshoe. "Yes, Mr. Hunter, I was referring to you," she replied coolly.

Kin gulped. Aunt Adrian looked pretty annoyed. And since when did anyone call Grandpa Hotshoe "Mr. Hunter"? It sounded strange.

Of course, it also sounded awfully strange to hear his own father referred to as "departed." Kin wasn't sure he'd ever get used to that. Kin, Laura, and Laptop had lived with Aunt Adrian since losing their parents more than a year ago in the tragic crash of World Wide Flight 888. Sometimes, though, it still felt to Kin as if it had all happened yesterday.

Aunt Adrian took a step toward Hotshoe, her keen gaze traveling from his thinning gray hair past his straggly gray beard to his well-worn blue coveralls. "If you had answered my calls, Mr. Hunter, I wouldn't have had to drive all this way to North Carolina just to speak to these children."

Kin exchanged a worried glance with his younger brother. Laptop shook his head somberly as he stood nearby with their little yellow dog, Scuffs. Kin noticed that his brother was clutching his Apricot 07 notebook computer so hard that his knuckles were white.

He's probably thinking the same thing I am, Kin thought grimly. *That Aunt Adrian's here to take us back to Boston with her.*

Kin couldn't think of anything worse. When he'd first come South to spend the summer with his grandfather, he hadn't been sure what to expect. Born and raised in California, he had always followed car racing because of Grandpa Hotshoe. He'd watched the big races on TV and read articles about the drivers in the newspaper, though he'd never actually been to a race in person. But from almost the first minute he'd set foot on a NASCAR race track, Kin had been hooked. The noise, the action, the speed, even the smells gave him a constant thrill of excitement. Traveling through the South with Grandpa Hotshoe, following the NASCAR circuit, was amazing enough. But then Kin had actually landed a job on a pit crew, working for Hotshoe's friend, Waddy Peytona. On Friday morning, less than three days from now, Kin would become an official member of Waddy's team. He couldn't wait.

Kin wasn't sure what Laptop thought about spending the summer with Grandpa Hotshoe. He usually seemed more interested in his Apricot 07 than anything else. Kin did know that Laura hadn't liked hanging around the track much at first—she'd made that perfectly clear, as she always did when she wasn't happy about something—but ever since she'd discovered her talent for music, she'd seemed much more content. She spent her days playing her mother's old guitar and helping Infield Annie, who ran a traveling homestyle restaurant on the circuit.

Aunt Adrian's big, quiet house in Boston seemed worlds away from all that. Kin watched as his aunt looked around the high school gym disapprovingly. "What kind of shenanigans have been going on here, anyway?"

Kin opened his mouth to explain, but Infield Annie beat him to it.

"These *shenanigans*," she said in her strong, deliberate voice, putting her hands on her ample hips, "happened to be a concert. And your niece was the star of the show."

"That's right, Aunt Adrian," Kin said nervously. "Laura's been playing Mom's old guitar. She sings, too."

"Singing, hmm?" Aunt Adrian said slowly.

Kin winced, suddenly realizing that Aunt

Adrian's tastes ran more to Bach and Beethoven than Sarah McLachlan or Garth Brooks.

"Really, it was great," Laptop put in eagerly. "You should have heard her, Aunt Adrian. She rocked."

Laura blushed. "But that's not all, Aunt Adrian," she added quickly, tugging on her shoulder-length blond hair. "We've all been having the best time! This is our new friend, Infield Annie. She's the best cook in the South. And Grandpa Hotshoe has been teaching us all about racing."

"Well, that's wonderful." Aunt Adrian smiled at the kids, revealing a quick glimpse of the warm heart beneath her chilly exterior. Then her smile faded again as she turned back to Hotshoe. "Still, it doesn't explain why I received no response to my messages. I must have called a dozen times, and I really—"

"Miz Adrian," Hotshoe interrupted, "with all due respect, I don't have time to play froggy and jump every time the phone rings. But that doesn't mean I'm not taking good care of my grandchildren. What's got your rpm's up, anyway?"

Kin gulped. His aunt and grandfather had spoken on the phone plenty of times, but this was the first time they'd met in person. Somehow Kin didn't think they were hitting it off too well so far.

Aunt Adrian hesitated, seeming taken aback by the question. "Well, I, uh . . . I knew next week was the twelfth. McKinley's sixteenth birthday. I didn't want to miss it."

Kin shook his head. "Not yet, Aunt Adrian," he said. "My birthday isn't until the twelfth of *September*. You're a couple of months early." He grinned weakly. "But if you want to give me some presents now, I don't mind."

Aunt Adrian closed her eyes. "Goodness." She sounded flustered. "I'm so sorry. I must have gotten confused."

Laura leaned toward Kin. "That's weird," she muttered under her breath as Infield Annie said something reassuring to Aunt Adrian. "Aunt Adrian never forgets things. What's wrong with her?"

Kin just shrugged. He didn't want his aunt to hear them. But Laura had a point—Aunt Adrian was acting pretty strange.

Aunt Adrian's eyes flew open and she glanced at her watch. "Well!" she said briskly, sounding a little more like her usual self. "I didn't realize how late it was getting. Shouldn't you children be in bed by now?"

"We were just on our way," Hotshoe answered for his grandchildren. "Where are you staying, Miz Adrian?"

"I sent Henri to find a suitable motel."

"Ornery?" Hotshoe repeated. "What kind of name is that?"

Laura, Kin, and Laptop all laughed. "Not *Ornery*, Grandpa," Laura explained. "It's *Henri*, pronounced 'Aahnn-ree.' That's French for 'Henry.'"

Grandpa Hotshoe grinned and winked, showing that he'd known it all along. Aunt Adrian didn't seem to notice.

"I don't know what's taking him so long." She checked her watch again.

"The motels are probably full of all the drivers and team members passing through town," Hotshoe said.

Seeing his aunt's confused look, Kin explained. "Tonight's concert was in honor of NASCAR families." He still didn't really understand why Aunt Adrian was here. Had she really driven all this way just to wish him a happy birthday?

"Worf! Worf!" Kin was distracted from his thoughts by Scuffs. A small, thin man with slicked-back black hair had just appeared in the gym door-way, and the little dog was sounding the alarm.

Aunt Adrian glanced toward the newcomer. "Ah, Henri, at last," she said with relief. "Any luck?"

"Finally I found two roomz," Henri said in a thick French accent, straightening his dark uni-form and giving Scuffs a disdainful look. "At ze Zudden Fallz Motel."

"Good." Aunt Adrian turned to Hotshoe and the kids. "Where are you staying? Perhaps we're at the same motel."

Hotshoe laughed. "I don't think so. We're stay-ing right here in the school parking lot. The towns-people were nice enough to let a lot of us NASCAR folks set up here."

"In a parking lot?" Aunt Adrian looked shocked.

"Sure." Hotshoe shrugged. "As good a place as any. The boys and I sleep in my RV . . . "

". . . and I sleep in Annie's Airstream trailer," Laura finished for him.

"RV. Trailer. My heavens," Aunt Adrian said faintly.

"Okay, kids," Annie said in her no-nonsense voice. She picked up Laura's guitar case with one hand and slung her other arm around Laura's shoulders. "Let's roll. It's late, and I'm sure your Aunt Adrian wants to talk to your Grandpa Hotshoe alone."

Kin nodded. "Come on, Laptop," he said, grabbing his younger brother's hand. "Grab that dog and let's go."

SMEDLEY'S SECRET

Laptop wriggled, shifting his computer from one arm to the other as he tried to get a better view. "What are they—"

"Sssh!" Kin hissed. "They'll hear us."

He crouched a little lower behind the bushes near the school doorway, watching the two adults who had just stepped out into the warm summer night. The air was filled with the lazy, peaceful sounds of crickets and frogs, and the moon cast a soft, silvery glow over the scene. Kin was annoyed that Laptop had tagged along, but there hadn't been any way to avoid it, not if he wanted to know what was going on. And he definitely did. He had to make sure his aunt wasn't planning to drag him back to Boston just when he was about to start his job with the pit crew.

Laptop was still craning his neck, trying to see the shadowy figures on the sidewalk twenty yards away. "Is she—hey Kin, I think she's *crying*!"

Laptop sounded amazed, and Kin didn't blame him. "Aunt Adrian?" he whispered back in disbelief. "I didn't think she even knew how to cry. She didn't even cry when . . ." His voice trailed off. He didn't want to get distracted thinking about his parents right now.

"Come on, let's get closer," Laptop urged quietly. "I can't hear what they're saying."

Kin nodded, and the two boys crept along behind the bushes, which formed a sort of informal hedge along the sidewalk. Soon they were only a few yards from the two adults.

"Forgive me, Mr. Hunter," Aunt Adrian was saying. "I've been under such a strain the last couple of days, I don't know what to do."

"How can I help?" Hotshoe asked. "What's the problem?"

"That's the problem, Mr. Hunter," she said. "I can't tell anyone what the problem is. Not even the police."

The police? Kin's eyes widened. He bent back a

few branches of the bush in front of him, trying to see Aunt Adrian's face. She wasn't crying anymore, but she looked more upset than he'd seen her since those terrible days just after the plane crash.

"I see," Hotshoe said thoughtfully. "Well, let's see what we can do. First of all, you'll have to stop calling me 'Mr. Hunter.' 'Hotshoe's' the name."

Aunt Adrian smiled faintly. "All right, Hotshoe. It's a deal. But only if you call me 'Adrian.'"

"Adrian it is," Hotshoe replied. "Now, you're going to have to tell someone what's going on, and I'm standing right here. So how about it? You can trust me."

Aunt Adrian pulled out a handkerchief and wiped her eyes. She hesitated for a moment, but then she nodded. "You're right. I have to tell someone or I'll go crazy." She took a deep breath. "As you know, my husband Smedley and I run an art gallery in Boston. I sent the kids to stay with you because Smedley and I were invited to contribute to a special show of American art in Paris."

Kin leaned forward a little more, not wanting to miss a word. Beside him, Laptop was chewing nervously on his thumbnail as he listened.

"Well, Smedley left with the painting last week,"

Aunt Adrian went on. "B-but he never got there."

Kin gasped as a vision of a plane plummeting toward the ocean popped into his mind. It was a vision that had haunted his nightmares for months after his parents died.

Hotshoe seemed to be thinking the same thing. "Not another accident!"

"No, no," Aunt Adrian said quickly. "The plane arrived safely. But the painting never made it to the museum. Neither did Smedley. At first I thought he'd been kidnapped. I was about to call the police when I received this." She pulled a videocassette out of her purse.

"What's on it?" Hotshoe asked.

Instead of answering, Aunt Adrian turned and walked toward her Mercedes-Benz limousine, which was parked nearby. Henri was standing on the far side of the car smoking a long, thin, smelly cigarette. At Aunt Adrian's approach, he tossed the cigarette away, hurried around, and opened the car's back door with a flourish.

"She's going to play that tape on the VCR in the limo," Laptop whispered urgently. "What should we do, Kin? If she shuts the door we won't be able to hear a thing!"

"Shhh!" Kin was more irritated than ever at having his little brother along. He was already trying to come up with a plan.

Laptop didn't bother to wait for him to figure it out. He parted the bushes and darted forward before Kin had time to react.

"Get back here!" Kin hissed. "Laptop!" He didn't dare speak above a whisper. Peering through the bushes, he saw his brother sneaking toward the limo. Grandpa Hotshoe was gallantly holding the door as Aunt Adrian climbed inside, so neither of them noticed the little boy as he dodged behind the car. Henri didn't either—the chauffeur had stepped away to light another smelly French cigarette. Laptop had chosen the perfect moment to get closer.

Letting out a frustrated sigh, Kin pushed his way through the bushes. He hated it when Laptop beat him to the punch like that. Sometimes it wasn't easy having a genius for a little brother.

By the time Hotshoe and Aunt Adrian were seated on the limo's plush seat, the two boys were crouched behind the rear tire, out of sight. Kin crossed his fingers, hoping the adults would leave the door open.

They did. If Kin leaned out and tilted his head

the right way, he could even see the media center inside the car. Aunt Adrian was leaning over to pop in the video.

Meanwhile, Hotshoe was glancing around the car. "Slick!" he said admiringly. "This is quite a vehicle." His voice was slightly muffled by the car, but Kin could still understand him perfectly.

"Thanks," Aunt Adrian replied distractedly, as she hit PLAY.

The TV screen flickered to life, displaying an elderly man with a shock of snow-white hair.

"Uncle Smedley," Laptop breathed. He was leaning out beside Kin, his eyes wide and curious.

Smedley was standing in front of a blank concrete wall holding a large, gilt-framed painting. Kin couldn't see it clearly, but he recognized the frame. He'd seen the painting hanging in his aunt and uncle's gallery many times. It was a scene showing two Civil War generals shaking hands.

"I've joined a gang of international art thieves," Smedley said, his high, reedy voice sounding a bit shaky. "Do not call the police, or we will destroy this painting. If you give us a million dollars, we will return it. You have one week to decide. We will be in touch soon with further instructions."

The screen went blank.

Wow, Kin thought. *This is huge!*

He could hardly believe what he had just heard. Stuffy old Uncle Smedley, an art thief? Could it really be true?

There was a moment of silence inside the car. Kin held his breath, wondering what would happen now.

Hotshoe spoke first. "Is that old painting really worth a million bucks?"

"It's worth far more," Aunt Adrian replied. "The painting doesn't belong to me. It's on loan from my old friend Jim Sheridan, a South Carolina businessman. I'm on my way there now to tell him what has happened."

"What if he wants you to go to the police?"

"I can't do that to Smedley. I have to give him a chance to return it. Maybe he's just having a midlife crisis."

Kin rolled his eyes, and Laptop snorted. Aunt Adrian was always defending Uncle Smedley, though Kin didn't understand why. As far as he could tell, Smedley had never laughed or cracked a joke or done anything the least bit interesting or fun in his entire life.

— — — — — — — — — — — — — — — — —

"Okay, then," Hotshoe said. He didn't seem to find Aunt Adrian's response strange, but then again, he'd never met Smedley. "I still have one question. Why did you come here? You're not planning to tell the kids about this, are you?"

"Of course not," Adrian said, sounding embarrassed. "To be honest, I . . . I'm not really sure why I came. I suppose I just wanted to see them. With Smedley gone, they're my only family."

"They're my family, too," Hotshoe said. "So I guess that means you and I are family. And family helps family, so you can count on me to help you however I can."

Kin saw his grandfather's legs swing out of the car. "Come on," he whispered to Laptop. "Let's get out of here. We can't let them see us—we have to get back to the trailer before Grandpa gets there."

For once Laptop didn't argue. He just nodded and followed as Kin dashed for the bushes.

When the two boys opened the door to their grandfather's RV, their sister was waiting for them. She was standing in the middle of the tiny living area with her arms folded across her chest.

"Where have you two been?" Laura demanded.

She'd suspected that Kin was up to something from the time she and Annie left the gym. Laura hated it when anything interesting happened without her knowing about it. That was why she'd crept out of the Airstream as soon as Annie turned on the shower. She'd been waiting almost twenty minutes and was starting to worry about getting back before Annie missed her.

Kin groaned. "What are you doing here?"

Laura didn't answer. She just waited. There was no way she was leaving the RV until she got some answers.

Kin scowled, but he didn't hold out for long. After checking outside to make sure that Grandpa was nowhere in sight, he quickly told his sister what he'd just seen and heard, with Laptop chiming in. By the time they finished, Laura had forgotten all about being annoyed.

"Man!" she exclaimed. "This is major news. Are you sure you heard them right? They weren't just joking around?"

"We told you." Laptop frowned. "We saw the video ourselves. This is for real."

Laura sank down onto her grandfather's favorite well-worn easy chair. "What should we do?"

"We should go to bed," Kin said. "What else can we do? It's not like we're going to come up with a million dollars. And it sounds like that's the only thing that might help."

SECRETS AND SCHEDULES

Laptop was dreaming about a computer that could print out million-dollar bills when a shuffling noise woke him. He sat up, rubbed his eyes, and squinted. Bright morning sunlight was pouring through the RV's windshield and side windows, spilling over into the berth above the driver's seat where Laptop slept.

He poked his head over the edge and saw his grandfather pulling on his shoes. Hotshoe glanced up and smiled. "Morning, kiddo," he said. "Sorry if I woke you."

"It's okay." Laptop swung his feet over the edge of the berth and hopped to the floor. He stood on tiptoes to reach back up and grab his Apricot 07 computer. Scuffs yawned and jumped down, too.

"I was just about to ease over to Annie's trailer and ask if maybe we can have breakfast at her place," Hotshoe said.

"Good idea," Laptop said, suddenly wide awake at the thought of Annie's delicious Southern cooking. His stomach growled as he imagined biting into one of her piping-hot biscuits. "I'll come, too."

"That's all right," Hotshoe said quickly. "I'll be back in a sec." He scooted out of the RV before Laptop could answer.

Laptop narrowed his eyes. But then he realized what Hotshoe was up to. *He's going to tell Annie what Aunt Adrian told him last night,* he thought. *Grandpa tells Annie everything.*

That made Laptop feel a little better. He didn't think much of most people's brains. As far as he could tell, a lot of them worked slower than the thick Southern molasses Annie used in her cooking. Most folks would be better off just relying on a computer to make their decisions for them.

But Annie was different. Even though Laptop had only met her recently, he could already tell she was sharper than a carton of tacks. She took everything in, digested it, and figured it out. Maybe she could figure out Aunt Adrian's problem, too.

Laptop tapped the hard plastic casing of the Apricot 07 thoughtfully. *Aunt Adrian has a week to decide what to do,* he mused. *If she doesn't tell the police, she'll lose everything. But if she does tell, Smedley will go to jail, and she may lose everything anyway.*

He flipped open the top of his computer and hit the switch that would bring it to life. "Maybe Annie can figure out a way to help Uncle Smedley," he murmured. "But just in case she can't, I'd better get to work on it myself."

"What's that?" Laptop asked when Annie passed him a bowl a short while later. He squinted suspiciously at the red-tinted liquid as Annie handed bowls to Laura, Kin, Hotshoe, Aunt Adrian, and Henri.

"Red-eye gravy," Annie said. "From country ham. Put some on a biscuit. You'll like it."

Aunt Adrian cautiously dipped one of Annie's homemade biscuits into the liquid and tasted it. Her eyes widened in surprised pleasure. "Mmm! It's very good."

Kin glanced at his aunt. Grandpa Hotshoe and Annie had invited Aunt Adrian and Henri to breakfast, and they were sitting with the others in the folding chairs Annie had set up in the grass along the edge of the parking lot. Aunt Adrian wasn't showing any sign that anything was wrong, though Kin knew better.

Still, he couldn't seem to concentrate on his aunt's problems for very long. He had other things on his mind—exciting things. "How long will it take us to get to Seabreeze Raceway?" he asked his grand father. "Junior said he'd probably be there by lunch-time tomorrow." Junior Peytona, Waddy's sixteen -year-old son, had been working on his father's pit crew since he was big enough to hoist a wrench. He and Kin had hit it off from the moment they'd met.

"Well, it's only Wednesday, and qualifying doesn't start until Friday afternoon," Hotshoe said. "We'll want to get there tomorrow to get settled in, but I thought we'd take a break today and have some fun." He winked at Laptop. "What say we hit the local amusement park after breakfast?"

Laptop blinked and dipped his biscuit into his gravy. "Sounds cool."

Kin held back a groan. He was itching to get to the track. "Yeah," he added weakly. "That'll be a blast, Grandpa."

"Good." Hotshoe reached for another biscuit and glanced at Aunt Adrian. "You and Henry there are welcome to join us."

"Thanks," Aunt Adrian said as Henri shot Hotshoe a disgruntled look. "But I've got to get down to South Carolina to . . . uh . . . visit an old friend. Perhaps we'll meet you in a few days."

Annie nodded and sipped her coffee. "One of the drivers offered to pull my Airstream to Seabreeze this afternoon. I'm going to head on down in my VW and set up my infield kitchen."

Kin wished he could go with her. But he didn't want to hurt his grandfather's feelings. He sighed. Seabreeze would just have to wait—for one more day, at least.

WELCOME TO SEABREEZE

Laura had never seen anything quite like the infield at Seabreeze Raceway. Even though it was only Thursday afternoon and race day wasn't until Sunday, there were already plenty of vehicles of all shapes and sizes parked there. There were even more campers, vans, trailers, pickups, and station wagons than there had been back at the track in Tennessee. During the drive down that morning, Hotshoe had explained that a lot of families planned their vacations around the NASCAR schedule, packing the kids in the car and setting up camp in the infield and every other spot of open space around the track.

"I guess that's what we're doing, too, huh?" Laptop had commented, looking up from his computer.

Grandpa Hotshoe had laughed. "For you it's a vacation, maybe," he'd teased. "For me, it's work." Hotshoe designed and sold camshafts, and his company, Merlin MixMaster, did a lot of business at the race track.

Laura wasn't sure the NASCAR circuit was exactly what she would have chosen for her vacation. Still, she had to admit that it had been a lot more fun than she'd expected so far.

Annie's Airstream had already been parked in the infield when they had arrived. Grandpa Hotshoe had parked his RV next to the big silver trailer and then hurried off. That was one thing Laura liked about being here—Grandpa didn't treat her like a baby who needed an adult to take care of her every second of the day, like Aunt Adrian did. He trusted her to take care of herself when he wasn't around. The only drawback was that she often had to look after Laptop as well.

She and Laptop helped Annie set up the tent that served as her portable restaurant. Kin had already wandered off to look for Junior and his other new friends from the pit crew. Laura was a little annoyed at that—she'd been hoping they would have a chance to discuss Aunt Adrian's problems this morning.

She sighed. She would have to settle for discussing it with Laptop. "Come on," she told her little brother after Annie shooed them out of her kitchen. "Let's find somewhere private. We've got things to talk about."

Laptop nodded. The two of them wandered through the infield, threading their way around vehicles, tents, picnic tables, and lawn chairs.

"There sure are a lot of people here," Laptop commented, clutching his computer to his chest as he walked.

"No kidding." Laura glanced around. "Check out those kids over there. What are they doing?" She stared past the rear bumper of an ancient Corvette. Just beyond it was an open, grassy section of the infield where nobody was parked. A boy and a girl about Laura's age were staring at the ground. The girl was holding a funny-looking object with a long handle—it looked sort of like the weed trimmer Aunt Adrian's gardener used to trim the grounds around her Boston home.

Laptop glanced at the pair. "Metal detector," he reported matter-of-factly.

Laura shot him an irritated glance. It was awfully annoying when her little brother knew something she didn't know. But she decided to let it pass this time. "What's it for?"

"See how they're sort of waving it over the ground?" Laptop pointed. "It beeps when it passes over anything made of metal, like coins or jewelry or . . ." His voice trailed off and his eyes widened. "Or buried treasure!"

"Oh." Laura took a step toward the two kids. "I wonder if they're finding anyth—"

"Laura!" Laptop tugged urgently at her sleeve. "This could be just what we need to help Aunt Adrian!"

"What are you talking about?"

Laptop was already marching toward the two kids. Laura had to scurry to catch up.

"Laptop!" she hissed. "What are you—"

It was too late. "Hi there," Laptop greeted the strangers. "I'm Laptop Travis and this is my sister, Laura. Is that a metal detector?"

The boy grinned, his white, even teeth gleaming in his tan face. "Laptop?" he repeated, jerking his head to toss his sandy-brown hair out of his hazel eyes. "What kind of name is that?"

Laura couldn't remember the last time she'd been so embarrassed. Leave it to Laptop to go charging up to total strangers and start acting like a big geek. "It's his nickname," she explained, her face flaming. "He's a computer freak. His real name's Larry."

"I think it's a cute nickname," the girl spoke up cheerfully. She had thick, curly brown hair and a round face. "It's nice to meet you, Laptop and Laura. I'm Jane Thompson and this is Eddie Harris." She peered at Laura. "I don't remember seeing you around before. Do you come to the races a lot?"

"Um, not exactly," Laura said. "We just came down from Boston to spend the summer with our grandfather."

"Grandpa Hotshoe used to be a race car driver," Laptop added.

"Hotshoe Hunter?" Jane asked. "He's your granddad?"

Eddie looked impressed. "My pop still talks about some of Hotshoe's big races. He's got an autographed picture of him on the wall in his den back home in Chicago."

"You came here all the way from Chicago?" Laura asked.

Jane jerked a thumb at Eddie. "He did," she said. "I'm from Florida." She giggled. "Eddie and I meet up every summer on the circuit, us and a few other kids we know, when our families come to the races. It's sort of our version of summer camp, I guess."

Laura noticed that Laptop was shifting his weight from foot to foot, looking impatient. He was staring at the metal detector, which Jane was still holding. "Is that yours?" he blurted out.

"This?" Jane glanced at the detector. "Sort of. It's my dad's. He lets me use it once in a while."

"Do you think I could borrow it?" Laptop asked eagerly. "You see, my Aunt Adrian and her husband run an art gallery in Boston, and . . . "

Laura couldn't believe it. Before she could react, Laptop was pouring out the whole story. She felt her face grow hot again as she wondered what Jane and Eddie would think. She wouldn't blame them if they thought Laptop was making it all up.

"Anyway," Laptop finished at last. "That's why we need to borrow that metal detector. Maybe we can find some real treasure buried under the fields around here, and our aunt can use it to pay that ransom and save Uncle Smedley from jail."

‒ ‒ ‒ ‒ ‒ ‒ ‒ ‒ ‒ ‒ ‒ ‒ ‒ ‒ ‒

Eddie looked doubtful, but Jane just giggled. "Treasure hunting? Sounds like fun," she said. "But I should probably warn you—the most my dad ever found in one day is fourteen dollars in change and an old set of silverware."

KENTUCKIANS NEVER TELL TALL TALES

The next day Kin awoke with a smile on his face.

It was Friday morning at last. His first day as a real pit crew member! He'd spent the previous afternoon hanging out with Junior in the garage area, meeting all sorts of people connected with racing. He couldn't wait to be a real part of their world—starting today.

He looked at the clock perched on the tiny table beside his narrow, drop-down bunk. "Yow!" he exclaimed, sitting up quickly. "Seven o'clock already."

He swung his feet over the edge of the bunk. As he pulled on his clothes he noted that Hotshoe was already gone, but Laptop was still asleep in his berth over the front seats of the RV. Scuffs was snoring softly at the young boy's side. That was good. As much as he liked the little dog, Kin didn't want Scuffs following him to the garage, not today. And he certainly didn't want Laptop tagging along.

He tiptoed over to the tiny kitchen area and gulped down two bowls of cereal without bothering to sit down. Then he was out the door, trotting through the labyrinth of RVs, camper trucks, vans, and old school buses that crowded the infield. He knew there would be even more vehicles parked there by Sunday—race day.

He hurried through the infield tunnel toward a small building with a ticket window and a sign reading NASCAR REGISTRATION.

"Excuse me," Kin said when he reached the window.

The man dozing inside came awake with a start. "What's up?"

"Do you have credentials for Kin Travis? Mr. Peytona said he'd leave them for me."

The man leaned forward. "You're Waddy's new crew member?"

"That's right."

"Well, I'll be! You're a young 'un." The man

shuffled through the papers piled on his desk. "Here we go. Gives your address as 'Hotshoe Hunter's RV.' You related to Hotshoe? His signature's already on this form as your guardian."

Kin nodded. "He's my grandfather."

The man handed Kin a clipboard with a long piece of paper on it. At the top were Kin's name and address. The rest of the page was covered in fine print. "Read this, son. Then sign at the bottom under your grandfather's name, I'll give you your pass, and you can be on your way."

"What am I signing?" Kin squinted at the tiny print.

"A release. In case something bad happens to you. We're counting on you to be careful so nothing does. By signing, your grandfather gave his promise that he'd look out for you, too. Got that?"

"Got it." Kin signed.

As soon as he had his pass in his hand, he took off. He ran back through the tunnel under the track and across the infield to a long, sliding gate in a chain-link fence. A security guard was standing by the gate. Kin slowed to a walk. He didn't want the guard to see how excited he was and take him for a rookie.

To Kin's disappointment, the guard barely glanced at his pass. Kin couldn't resist. "I'm in Waddy Peytona's pit crew," he said. "Just signed on this morning."

The guard smiled. "That's fine, son. That's real fine."

Kin hurried toward the long garage that covered the nose-to-nose double row of race cars and crews.

A tall, blond girl caught his eye and he paused. But as soon as he got a good look at her face, he saw that she was a stranger.

He frowned, realizing that for a split second he'd thought the blond girl was Teresa Peytona, Junior's twin sister. Kin had met Teresa back in Tennessee, and he hadn't been able to get her out of his mind since.

"Get over it, man," he muttered to himself. "You can't let yourself get distracted. Not on your first day on the job."

He continued on his way, doing his best to forget about Teresa. As he walked down the length of the garage, almost every car he saw was on a jack stand. The hoods were all up, like gaping metal mouths clamoring for attention.

What if aliens suddenly dropped in from outer space? Kin wondered with a secret grin. *They'd probably think all race cars come with people's legs sticking out from under them.*

In addition to several sets of legs sticking out from all angles, most of the cars had several people leaning over their engine compartments. Some also had someone leaning through the driver's window, presumably doing something with the seat or gearshifter or gauges.

Fascinated by the activity all around him, Kin found himself walking more and more slowly as he tried to take it all in. But finally he realized he was wasting time. He glanced at his watch, then looked around for the familiar blue and yellow hood of Waddy's Ford Taurus.

He didn't see it, so he looked for someone to ask. A young man with a crew cut and a friendly smile was walking by. He looked like a pit crew member to Kin, who held out a hand to stop him.

"Excuse me," Kin said. "Could you tell me where—"

He gasped as he noticed the name patch on the young man's chest. It was Jeremy Mayfield, one of NASCAR's superstar drivers!

"Can I help you?" Mayfield asked politely in his warm Kentucky accent.

"Um . . ." Kin did his best to pull himself to gether and act cool, not wanting to look like an idiot in front of the driver. "Yeah. Thanks. I'm looking for number eighty-two."

"Waddy Peytona? You one of his new guys?"

"Sure am," Kin said proudly.

"I'm heading that way. I'll walk you over," Mayfield said. "My name's—"

"I know who you are, Mr. Mayfield," Kin said quickly. "I'm Kin Travis."

"Hotshoe's grandson?"

"That's right."

"Welcome to the NASCAR family," Mayfield said. "Waddy's quite a driver. Hey, did you ever wonder how he got number eighty-two?"

Kin shrugged, realizing he'd never given it any thought. "I guess I figured he just drew it or something."

"There's a story behind it." Mayfield glanced at Kin with a twinkle in his eye. "I'm a Kentuckian like Waddy, so I know the story well. Want to hear it?"

"Sure." Kin could hardly believe a famous driver was walking along talking to him like they were the best of buddies.

"Waddy was only sixteen when he first started racing," Mayfield said. "He was driving a hobby stocker at a dirt track better known for its home-made ice cream than for its races. One night an older driver figured he might have a chance of beating Waddy if he got Waddy sick before the race. So he bet Waddy five dollars that he couldn't eat a quart of ice cream all by himself. Waddy said he wasn't sure. Could the man give him a little while to make up his mind? The man said sure, and Waddy left.

"In about twenty minutes Waddy came back and said he'd take the bet. The man went to the con-cession stand and came back with a heaping quart of strawberry, Waddy's favorite, and Waddy sat down and ate it all, then collected his five dollars.

"After the race—which Waddy won without getting sick—the man asked Waddy why he had left before taking the bet. Had he gone off some-where to throw up and empty his stomach? Waddy said no, nothing like that. Since he couldn't afford to take a chance on a five dollar bet, he'd gone over to the concession stand to see if he could eat a quart of ice cream. When he found out he could, he came back and took the bet.

"For a long time after that, Waddy was called 'Ate Two,' and that's why he asks NASCAR for the number eighty-two every year."

"Really?" Kin grinned, trying to imagine short, stocky, energetic Waddy hunched over a quart of strawberry ice cream.

"One thing us Kentuckians never do," Mayfield said, "is tell tall tales. There's your car over there."

With a smile and a handshake, he was gone.

THREE *L'S* PLUS ONE

Kin saw a large yellow number two with a blue border. It was on the half-open back door of the last hauler in line. On the other door, the one that opened away from him, was the numeral eight. Waddy Peytona, a stocky man with bright, alert eyes narrowed into a perpetual squint, was standing nearby talking to a couple of other men from the crew. His son Junior, who looked just like him, was tinkering with a wrench near the back end of the hauler, a Talladega Superspeedway cap perched jauntily over his dark, wavy hair.

Kin gave Junior a quick wave, then hurried over to Waddy, eager to get started. "Good morning, Mr. Peytona," he said cheerfully. "I'm here."

Waddy frowned and looked at his watch.

"Yeah. And you're an hour and a half late. The garage opened at six."

Kin gulped. Suddenly he noticed that the other crew members—crew chief Cope, Carl the suspension expert, Tach the head engine mechanic, even Junior—had stopped working to listen.

"Don't want to come down too hard on you, boy, right off the bat." Waddy rubbed his neck with one strong, stubby-fingered hand. "But if you're going to be part of this crew, you've got to be a full part. When we work, you work. And we start work when that gate out there opens. Understand?"

"Y-yes. I mean, sorry. I mean—" Kin took a deep breath. "We, uh, I mean last night I was, uh, I didn't . . . "

Waddy shut him up with a shake of his head. "Don't matter what you did or what you didn't. It's your responsibility to be here on time. Got that?"

Kin nodded. "I'll try to make up for it, Mr. Peytona. I really will. I want to be the best tire changer you've ever had, next to Junior."

Waddy sighed and put a hand on Kin's shoulder. "Junior told me you wanted to be a tire changer. I'm afraid you're not quite ready for that, son. It takes years to make a good tire changer."

Kin felt his heart sink even lower. "But I know I can do it," he protested. "I mean, Junior can do it. And I'm almost the same age he is."

Waddy shook his head. "It's not a matter of age, or even size. You have to be strong. Now, you and Junior are around the same height. But take a close look at him sometime. He outweighs you by twenty pounds, and most of that's muscle. He's been lifting tires and rims and parts and jacks since he was big enough to walk. He's grown up doing this. How much hard work have you done up to now? Not much, I bet. Stick out your hands."

Kin obeyed. As Waddy reached to grab his hands, Kin saw what he meant. Next to Waddy's large, callused hands, Kin's own hands looked thin and pale and weak.

Waddy shook his head again. "See what I mean?" He let Kin's hands drop. "Do you know what a tire weighs?"

Junior came forward, shooting Kin a sympathetic look. "Daddy's right," he said. "A NASCAR tire has an outer casing—that's what you see—and an inner liner, which you don't. Sort of a tire within a tire."

"That's right," Waddy said. "The whole shootin'

match, tire, inner tire, and rim, with lug nuts already glued on it, weighs about seventy pounds. You following me so far?"

Kin nodded numbly.

"Good, 'cause I'm coming to the hard part. Which is that, like you as much as I do, it wouldn't be fair to you or the rest of the team to let you try to change a tire during a race."

Kin clenched his jaw hard, trying to keep it from trembling. He was so surprised and disappointed that he was afraid he might start crying—and that was the last thing he wanted to do right now, in front of these men.

"Isn't there something I can do, Mr. Peytona?" he asked.

"I'm sure we can find something," Waddy said. "I did ask you to join my team, didn't I? Now, have you heard of the three *R*'s?"

"You mean reading, writing, and 'rithmetic?"

"Right," Waddy said. "Now, here are Waddy's three *L*'s—look, listen, and learn. What I want you to do is climb up on that workbench there"— he pointed to a waist-high bench near the car—"and just sit there and keep your eyes and ears open. Look, listen, learn. Got it?"

"Got it." Kin still felt a little disappointed. It didn't sound as though he was going to be an active part of the team at all, at least not anytime soon. Still, if he hung around and paid attention, maybe Waddy would give him something to do before long.

Waddy scratched his chin. "Look, listen, learn," he repeated. "Hmm. I just thought of a fourth *L* for you, son—leap to it. That's what I want you to do if somebody tells you to do something. Understand?"

"Absolutely!" Kin felt his heart lift. "I'll do anything you want."

"Good. Then if you pay attention, maybe you can handle the catch can during the race."

"The catch can?" Kin repeated.

Waddy nodded. "You use it to catch any overflow from the fuel cell during refueling. NASCAR requires it."

Junior grinned and flexed his muscles. "Yeah," he joked. "And don't worry. The catch can only weighs about half a pound."

Everyone laughed, and Kin joined in. He didn't even care that they were making fun of him, sort of. He was too glad to be there.

BREAKFAST WITH THE STARS

Laura woke up in Annie's Airstream thinking about Uncle Smedley. What had made him do it? How could a person just go and do something so unexpected and devious after a lifetime of being proper, upright, and totally boring? It didn't seem right.

Laura lay in her bunk, staring at the smooth, curved metal ceiling above her. She had never paid much attention to Uncle Smedley, even though she'd lived in the same house with him for a year. That was the thing about a big old house like Aunt Adrian's—you could wander around the spacious rooms and long halls for days and hardly see the other people you were living with. Not like this trailer.

Laura smiled and sat up, glancing around the Airstream. Like everyone else, she'd been surprised when Annie had first invited her in. The outside of the trailer looked exactly like half a dozen other Airstreams out there in the infield—sleek, shiny, gleaming in the hot Carolina sunshine. The inside was another story. Annie collected American textiles, and the interior of her rolling home was layered in warm, cozy quilts, cheerful curtains, and handmade hooked rugs in a jumble of colors. Even after just a few days, it already felt like home to Laura.

She rolled out of bed and padded across the floor toward the kitchen, yawning. Annie seemed to be up early, as usual—Laura figured she was already over at the restaurant dishing out breakfast to early risers.

After helping herself to a glass of orange juice from the half-size refrigerator, Laura perched at the trailer's tiny table. For a second she couldn't understand why her leg muscles groaned in protest, but then she remembered. She and Laptop had spent hours the day before with their new friends, searching the ground with that stupid metal detector. They'd bent and dug each time the machine bleeped, but in the end they hadn't found anything more than a couple of coins and an old tin can.

She sighed. Jane and Eddie had seemed eager enough to help them go on searching today, but Laura wasn't looking forward to it. No matter what Laptop thought, there was no way they were going to uncover anything valuable enough to pay that ransom. In fact, there just didn't seem to be any way to help Aunt Adrian out of this mess at all. Maybe they should just leave it up to the adults.

After slipping on her shoes, Laura headed for the door. Annie would be needing her help over at the restaurant. Breakfast was always one of her busiest times.

About nine-thirty, just as Laura finished dishing out a platter of ham and biscuits to a family from Delaware, she glanced toward the door and saw a tall, ruggedly handsome man entering the restaurant. She had no trouble picking out the name embroidered above the upper left pocket of his blue and white uniform—Rusty Wallace.

She had heard Kin talking excitedly about Rusty Wallace often enough to know that this man was a top NASCAR driver. She gazed at him, a little impressed in spite of herself. Even though she wasn't that interested in car racing, she had to admit that it was kind of exciting, hanging around the track and seeing all these famous drivers in person.

Suddenly she saw that Rusty Wallace was looking back at her. She blushed, embarrassed to be caught staring. But he smiled and came toward her.

"You're the girl who sang at the NASCAR families' benefit the other night, aren't you?" he asked.

"That's me." Laura was thrilled that he had recognized her. She held out her hand politely. "I'm Laura Travis. My stage name is Mountain Laurel."

Wallace shook her hand. "Glad to meet you," he said. "My rival and friend Dale Earnhardt is on his way here, and he likes your singing, too. I wonder if you would sing us a song to start the day?"

Laura smiled, suddenly feeling bashful. When she'd started playing the guitar Annie had given her, the one that had belonged to Mrs. Travis when she was a girl, it had just seemed like a good way to feel closer to her mother. But now it seemed everyone wanted to hear Laura play and sing.

— — — — — — — — — — — — — — — —

"Sure," she said. "I'd be honored, Mr. Wallace."

She hurried behind the counter. Carefully lifting the old Wabash Cannonball guitar out of its case, she ran her fingers lightly over the strings. Then she carried the guitar out front.

Just then another man in a driver's uniform entered the crowded restaurant. Even though the morning was cloudy, the driver wore sunglasses. He moved like someone in a hurry, but he stopped to autograph anything and everything—programs, newspapers, hats, even napkins—that his fans handed to him.

"Dale Earnhardt," Annie whispered to Laura. "I reckon that's one reason NASCAR's so popular. The drivers aren't too big for their britches. Even the great ones, like Dale and Rusty."

Laura hadn't thought about that before, but she had to agree with Annie. Everyone she had met so far on the NASCAR circuit had been unassuming and friendly, including the big-name drivers.

She settled herself near the counter and started to play. Her fingers flew over the strings, and her voice poured out of her throat, rich and true. The two drivers smiled appreciatively as they sat down with the food Annie had handed them, and the other customers tapped their feet and nodded their heads in time with the mellow beat.

Laura played two or three songs before Dale Earnhardt glanced at his watch and stood up. "That girl sings a lot better than you and me drive, Rusty!" he joked. "But hurry up and let's get going. The track opens for practice in five minutes."

With a word of thanks to Laura, the two men were gone. But the other customers were begging for more music. Laura glanced at Annie. She wouldn't mind singing and playing all day, but Annie had only recently started letting her help serve her customers. Laura didn't want to back out on that work now.

Annie winked as she dished up another plate of ham and biscuits. "What are you waiting for, darlin'?" she asked Laura. "Your fans are waiting."

TAKING TEMPS

At about the same time, Kin was helping the team push Waddy's car out from its garage stall. It was just a big, heavy hunk of metal, about as exciting as a grocery cart.

Then Waddy started it.

The Taurus exploded into life with a crackling, eardrum-piercing roar. Eight cylinders pumping pure power, eager to hit the track.

"Awesome," Junior whispered.

Kin agreed. He felt a thrill run through him. To be this close to something so powerful, to feel the ground shake, to smell the fumes and feel the heat from the exhaust—it was like nothing he'd ever experienced before.

And he was a part of it!

This blue and yellow Ford with the big number eighty-two on its top and sides, this awesome car leaving them in the dust as it roared off toward the track, was Kin's car now. Whenever it was on the track or mentioned on TV or talked about by someone in the infield or in the stands, Kin had a connection to it.

Kin watched until the car was out of sight, then glanced around at the faces of Junior and Cope and Carl and the others. Did they feel it, too? He suspected they did. Number eighty-two wasn't just Waddy Peytona's car. It was *their* car. All of theirs.

As he followed the team toward pit road, Kin saw that the backs of their shirts were streaked with sweat. They had been working hard all morning, with the pace getting faster and faster as practice time came closer.

"Do this, do that," crew chief Cope had been saying all morning, often to two or three people at once, pointing here and there with his long, skinny fingers. "We can't be the last ones out for practice." He had paused at one point to watch several gray-suited crew members walk by their area. After they were gone, he'd run his hand through his bright red hair and muttered, "We sure can't let that Gray bunch beat us!"

Kin was pretty sure he was the only one who'd been standing close enough to hear him. Junior had told him that the Gray racing team's sponsor was anonymous, that they always finished their races without coming in either first or last. Kin had seen for himself that the crew members all looked alike, with short gray hair and gray eyes. He'd never gotten a good look at the Gray driver, but he had seen enough to know that he dressed all in gray, too, just like his crew.

Kin and the rest of Waddy's team made it to pit road just in time to see the Taurus come by on its first practice lap. As Waddy streaked down the front straightaway low, Dale Earnhardt and Rusty Wallace, running nose-to-tail, roared by him on the high side.

"They passed him so easy," Kin said to Junior. "What's wrong?"

"Nothing." Junior shrugged. "Daddy's just taking it easy. Watching his gauges and making sure everything looks okay. Letting the oil and water come to temperature slowly. He'll probably come in and have us check for leaks before he stomps on it. No sense taking chances."

Kin nodded, wondering if he would ever know as much about this stuff as Junior did. *Look, listen, learn,* he told himself.

After a few more laps, Waddy slowed and turned down pit road just as Junior had predicted. As he came to a stop he stuck his hand through the mesh over the side window and pointed—first toward the front, then down at the ground.

Cope and Tach were already stepping over the wall toward the front of the car. Carl and Junior were hopping over, too. As Kin watched from his position on the top of the wall, the two of them hit the ground and slid under the car to take a look. Kin was itching to be down there with them, but he knew better. He didn't want to get in the way.

Cope removed the hood pins and held open the hood while Tach walked around the engine compartment prodding, poking, and just looking. Finally he nodded, and Cope put the hood down.

Carl and Junior stood up and nodded to Cope. The crew chief stepped away from the car and gave Waddy a thumbs-up. "Copacetic!" he called. Waddy nodded back from the driver's seat. A second later, with a squeal of tires, the blue and yellow Taurus accelerated down pit road toward turn one.

Junior walked toward the wall, smiling and rubbing his hands together. "All right!" he called to Kin. "Now we can get with it. No sign of oil under the car. No transmission or rear-end leak. And I'm sure the motor well was clean, or Tach wouldn't have let Daddy go back out."

Cope wandered over and put his right foot up on the wall a few yards from Kin and Junior. He grabbed a clipboard that Kin hadn't noticed sitting there and strapped it to his thigh, as if it were a table. Kin saw two stopwatches attached to the clipboard, one in each upper corner. He gave Junior a questioning look.

"Cope's going to time each hot lap Daddy makes," Junior explained. "First lap on one watch, second on the other. During the second lap he can write down the first, then reset it to record the third lap, and so on."

Kin nodded. "I get it," he said. "Makes a lot of sense."

Junior gestured toward Cope, who was putting on a set of headphones complete with a microphone held close to his mouth by a curved loop of stiff wire. "Meanwhile, he and Daddy can talk over their radios and figure out where the groove might be. Daddy can try running high, running low, maybe going in low and letting the car drift, or maybe trying to pinch it down. Lots of things." He grinned. "Teresa always says drivers and mechanics have to worry about more symptoms and possibilities than doctors do." He shrugged. "But anyhow, the clock will tell them which groove is fastest."

"I see." Kin was suddenly having trouble paying attention to what Junior was telling him. Why did he have to mention Teresa? Kin hadn't thought about her all morning. Well, not much, anyway.

Junior didn't notice his distraction. "Check it out!" he said, pointing to the track. "The Gray car's coming out. They're almost always the last ones on the track." He pulled a stopwatch out of his pocket. "Think I'll time them—not that it'll do any good. They almost always sandbag."

Kin had heard that term around the track, but he wasn't sure exactly what it meant. "Does that mean they don't go as fast as they could?"

"You got it," Junior said. "*Sandbagging* means holding back. A driver, or a team for that matter, doesn't run as fast as it can. Kind of lulls the other teams into thinking their own cars are better than they really are."

A moment later Waddy's car roared past again. "Looks like he's going faster than before," Kin commented.

"Still not flat out, though," Junior said. "He's waiting for a hole. When one opens up, he'll stand on it. He needs a gap to run in all alone, so he won't be slowed by anybody, or pulled along in a draft. He and Cope want to find out how the car runs by itself, like he'll be running this afternoon during qualifying. In practice tomorrow, assuming we qualify today, we'll want to run in traffic, the way we'll have to in the race. You don't always set up a car for the race the way you set it up for qualifying."

Two laps later, Waddy came down the front straightaway flat out. Instead of looking smooth and stable, the way it had looked on its slower laps, the car was rocking from side to side, buffeted by the wind it was creating and also shaken by the powerful engine under its hood, which was straining to pull it forward.

Kin was having trouble keeping track of the number of laps Waddy had gone. There was so much to look at, listen to, learn all around him. He watched the rest of the crew. He checked out the other cars as they zoomed past.

He thought it was about ten hard laps later when Cope suddenly stepped down from the wall, pulled off his headset, and barked out, "Heads up, everybody. He's coming in."

Junior and the others ran to the wall, looking eagerly down pit road. Kin could tell they were ready to swing into action as soon as the car arrived. He only wished he had something to do as well.

He glanced around. Most of the crew members were just standing there waiting, empty-handed. But Carl was holding a small black box in his left hand. It was about the size of a remote control for a TV set. In his right hand was a long, thick needle, which was attached to the black box by a wire. Kin had no idea what it was for, but he planned to look, listen, and learn to find out.

Waddy drove into the pit and brought the car to an abrupt halt. Before the wind and dust had even begun to settle, Carl hopped over the wall. He dropped to one knee by the right front tire and jabbed the long needle he was holding into the tread.

Kin gasped. What in the world was Carl doing? He was going to puncture the tire! He glanced over at Cope, expecting to hear him yell. But Cope was watching calmly. As Carl looked at the little black box and started calling out numbers, Cope jotted them down on his clipboard.

For a moment Kin felt foolish. There was so much he didn't know about this sport. *But I'm learning*, he reminded himself. *That's all I can do.*

He watched as Carl jabbed the tire in three places, then hopped up and hurried over to the left front tire. Carl jabbed the needle in again, looked at the black box, and called out a number to Cope. Within minutes he had repeated the process with both rear tires as well. When he was finished, he backed up and moved over to the pit wall while Junior and the others checked over other parts of the car.

Cope studied his clipboard for a moment, then walked over to the driver's side window. He leaned down and held the clipboard out so Waddy could see it.

Kin glanced at Carl, who was leaning on the wall nearby. "Um, what was that all about?" he asked tentatively. He hated to bother the crew while they were working, but Carl didn't look busy. Besides, if he didn't ask questions, how was he going to learn anything? "Why didn't that needle thing puncture the tires?"

Carl glanced at him and chuckled. "It's not a needle, son, it's a digital thermometer." He held up the black box so Kin could see it, and flipped a switch. A red number eighty-four appeared in its small window. "I stick the probe into the rubber, but not all the way through. The idea is to see how hot the tire is in different places."

"Are you afraid it'll get too hot and blow?"

"Not really," Carl explained in his slow, measured drawl. "Oh, a tire can get too hot, for sure. But what I was doing was measuring the temperature at four places, from the outside to the inside edge."

Junior had wandered toward the wall just in time to hear what Carl was telling Kin. "And he was doing it quickly," he chimed in, "before the tires cooled off, so we know what it was like on the track." He hoisted himself over the wall. So did Carl and the others. A moment later Waddy drove off toward the track once again.

Kin watched him go, trying to sort out all the

interesting things Carl was telling him. "Why do you need to know something like that?"

If Carl thought it was a stupid question, he didn't let on. "To get a car to stick in the turns, we want to have as much rubber as possible in contact with the track. The more rubber, the better the car sticks. When the car goes into a turn, the top of the tire tries to 'tip' over the bottom. The inside edge tends to roll up, and the outside edge tends to roll under. On a race car we compensate for that by tipping the tire to start with. That angle we call 'camber.'"

"Good morning, everyone!"

Kin didn't have to turn his head to find out who had interrupted Carl's explanation. He would have recognized that voice anywhere. Teresa.

He glanced over his shoulder as she approached. "Uh, hey there, Teresa," he said, hoping that his voice didn't give away how flustered he felt all of a sudden. For a while there, he had actually succeeded in putting her violet eyes and her honey-blond ponytail out of his mind. But now here she was, standing beside him, smiling that smile that made his knees go wobbly, and he couldn't seem to think of anything else.

"Howdy, Miss Teresa," Carl said. He glanced at Kin. "Ahem. You want to learn about camber or not, boy?" His voice sounded curt, but he was smiling. He gave Kin a slow, playful wink.

Kin felt his face grow hot. Were his feelings really that obvious? Could Teresa herself see the effect her arrival was having on him, or didn't girls notice that sort of thing? "Uh, sure, Carl," he said, doing his best to sound casual. "You were saying?"

"Mind if I listen in, too?" Teresa asked Carl. She jerked her head toward Junior. "Whenever I ask Mr. Know-it-all there, he acts like I couldn't understand this stuff even if he mixed it up in a blender and poured it in my ear."

Junior rolled his eyes. "Yeah, right," he said. "That's just because she can't ever seem to listen for more than ten seconds without interrupting."

Carl chuckled. "Listen away," he told Teresa. "Anyway, as I was saying, when the car goes into a left turn, there's tremendous pressure on the right front tire. The track tries to hold on to the bottom of the tire, and the weight of the car tries to tip the tire over at the top. To allow for that, we tip the tire inward to start with. Going down the straightaway, the car's actually running on the inside edge of the

tire. If we've set it right, when the car goes into the turn the tire will tip and distort just enough for the bottom to be running flat on the track, giving us the most rubber possible in the turn where we need it. Heck, down the straightaway we could run on a bicycle tire."

"I get it, I think," Kin said. "But I still don't understand what the temperatures have to do with it."

"If the tire's hot on the outside edge, that means it's running on the outside in the turn, and you don't have enough camber," Carl explained. "If it's hot on the inside, you have too much."

"Tell them about caster," Junior said.

"Isn't that a kind of oil?" Teresa asked innocently.

"Very funny," Junior said sarcastically.

When Kin glanced at Teresa, he saw a twinkle in her violet eyes. He suspected she actually knew exactly what caster was, though he himself had only the vaguest idea.

"Caster's more complicated," Carl drawled. "Maybe I can fill you in on that when we have more time." He nodded down pit road. Waddy's Taurus was coming toward them again. "Right now we've got work to do."

PERCOLATOR, DRIP, AND RACING GRIND

Laptop sat in the shade of the Gregson Racing hauler, his back against one of the truck's big tires, his Apricot 07 on his lap.

He'd been following Hotshoe from team to team all day. They had met a few drivers, which had been kind of fun. But Hotshoe was mostly interested in talking to the engine builders, either trying to sell them a new camshaft or finding out how the one he'd already sold them was performing. Laptop couldn't really follow most of what they talked about—Grandpa Hotshoe seemed to wave his hands around a lot, using funny words like *dwell* and *duration* and *grind* and *lift*.

At the moment, his grandfather was talking a mile a minute to a big man in black jeans. Laptop wasn't paying much attention. He had spent every spare moment of the last hour or two searching the Internet for information on treasure hunting. Yesterday had been a good start, but he was going to have to get organized if he wanted to find anything decent in time to meet Uncle Smedley's demands.

He looked up from the keyboard for a moment, thinking about Uncle Smedley. He really didn't know much about the man he'd been living with for the past year. He was Aunt Adrian's third husband; he was an expert in American art; he didn't like butter on his toast. That was about the extent of what Laptop knew.

He shrugged. It didn't matter. He didn't have to figure out why Uncle Smedley had done what he'd done—he just had to find a way to help Aunt Adrian. He liked Aunt Adrian, even though he hadn't been sure he was going to at first. Under that cold, haughty exterior she was kind and sensitive, with a dry, intelligent sense of humor.

Laptop returned his attention to the computer screen in front of him. He had just opened an e-mail from KiwiJoe, a pen pal in New Zealand. Laptop had computer buddies all over the world—Russia, Scotland, Canada, Africa, even the South Pole. Last night, after Kin and Grandpa were already snoring away in the RV, he'd sent a general e-mail message to all of them asking for information on buried treasure in this part of the American South. He figured if anyone had any good tips, he'd have that much better chance of finding what he needed.

Unfortunately, KiwiJoe didn't have much to contribute. He had just written to wish Laptop luck. Hitting a key to delete the message, Laptop let one hand drop to Scuffs's sun-warmed yellow fur. The dog sighed and snorted in his sleep as Laptop scratched absently behind his ears.

What now? Laptop wondered. For once, he was itching to put his computer away. He had already filed all the treasure-hunting information he'd found on the Internet in his computer's memory banks. Now what he really wanted to do was find Jane and Eddie and get back to work with that metal detector. But Grandpa had insisted on dragging him along as he went about his business, and Grandpa was a lot harder to slip away from than Kin or Laura.

"Ready to eat, kiddo?"

Laptop glanced up. His grandfather was smiling down at him.

"Finally," Laptop said with a groan. He snapped

his computer shut and climbed to his feet.

When he looked at Grandpa Hotshoe again, the old man was frowning a little sadly. "Sorry, son. I probably should've left you with Annie and Laura, where you at least might meet some kids your own age." He shrugged. "It can't be very exciting for you, hanging around a geezer like me, listening to me do my business. I guess I didn't think about it before— I like having you tag along." He placed one big hand on Laptop's shoulder. "I never realized how quickly you three young 'uns would grow on me."

Laptop swallowed hard, suddenly feeling guilty. He hadn't meant to hurt his grandfather's feelings. "I didn't mean that," he said quickly. "I like tagging along, Grandpa. I just meant I was getting hungry."

Hotshoe didn't look convinced. "It's okay, boy," he said gruffly. "You don't have to make nice with me."

"It's true," Laptop insisted as the two of them started walking slowly in the direction of Infield Annie's, with Scuffs padding sleepily behind them. "Watching you work is interesting." He decided the best way to make Grandpa Hotshoe forget what he'd said was to distract him. And the best way to do that was to get him talking about cars. "Actually,

Grandpa, I've been meaning to ask you. How'd you get started in the camshaft business, anyway?"

Grandpa Hotshoe smiled down at him and tousled his hair. "It was my second choice," he said. "When I first stopped driving, I got out of racing altogether and opened a parts store back in Tennessee. Me being a famous—well, nearly famous—race car driver, I figured folks would come from miles around to do business with me. Especially my old friends."

Laptop was relieved. His ploy had worked. His grandfather had that faraway look in his eyes—the look he always got when he talked about the old days. "And did they?" he asked.

"Oh, people came all right." Hotshoe waved one hand in the air. "A few became loyal customers. But most just came to shoot the breeze, hear tall tales, and brag about how they could've been a race car driver if it wasn't for their wives or their folks or whatever. When it came time to actually buy something, they'd head down the road to the discount stores that could offer lower prices than I could."

"That's kind of rotten," Laptop commented.

Hotshoe nodded. "Well, that's why I got out of the parts business," he said. "Didn't like it much anyway. I missed the smell of oil and hard grease and gasoline. I missed the sound of engines. So I looked for some way I could make a living and still be around the track. I started this camshaft business about six years ago. Two young guys in my Merlin MixMaster shop in Charlotte make camshafts for about fifteen of these race teams and for a bunch of speed shops around the country."

"And you design them," Laptop said. "Right?"

"Design and sell them," Hotshoe replied. "I go around to race tracks or shops—I like the tracks best—and try to get new customers while I check on old ones. I find out how our cams have performed and what the teams might want to try next. In racing, everybody's always trying to go faster, so they experiment with everything from the crankshaft alloy to the sparkplug gap to the camshaft lift. That's where I come in. I help them try to come up with a cam that'll give better performance. It's like everything else in racing. It's both a science and an art."

Laptop nodded thoughtfully. He hadn't really thought about what his grandfather did that way. "Cool," he pronounced.

Hotshoe looked pleased. "You know what a camshaft does, don't you, kiddo?"

Laptop had no idea, but he wasn't about to admit that. "Sure," he said with a grin. He gestured to the dog trotting along beside him. "I know all about it. But Scuffs doesn't. Maybe you'd better tell him."

Scuffs looked up at the sound of his name. "Worf," he barked.

Hotshoe chuckled, then pretended to address the dog. "Well, Scuffs, the camshaft is the thing in the engine that operates the valves. It's got lobes on it—little bumps, or 'cams'—that push against the valve stem, one for each valve. Each cylinder has both an intake and an exhaust valve, and the camshaft times when the valves open and close. You can change the way an engine performs by changing how long a valve stays closed and when it starts to open. The shape of the cam, or the 'grind,' determines all that. On short tracks you want sudden power, for acceleration. That calls for one type of grind. On long tracks, you want top end, high rpm. That's another grind."

"I couldn't have explained it better myself," Laptop announced as they reached Infield Annie's restaurant. He looked down at Scuffs. "Got it, boy?"

PRACTICE DOESN'T ALWAYS MAKE PERFECT

After Carl had checked the tires, Kin had lost track of what the others on the team were doing. But Junior filled him in, telling him that they'd "added more bite" to the car, which Waddy had said was loose. Waddy had made four laps under Cope's watchful eye and careful timing.

But instead of making the car faster, the change had made it slower. So the Peytona Team began trying other changes: alternately increasing and decreasing tensions on the springs around the car; adjusting the track bar up and down; changing air pressure in one tire and then another. They even hurried back to the garage area and made a complete change of springs.

Some time later Junior wiped his brow with the

back of one hand, leaving a splotch of grease across his forehead. "Nothing's working," he told Kin dejectedly. "Nothing we do seems to help."

Kin didn't know what to say. He wished he had some ideas to suggest. But so far, the best he could seem to do was stay out of the way and try not to look like an idiot in front of Teresa, who was still hanging around.

"Too bad," Teresa told her brother. She glanced at her watch. "Practice is over, huh?"

Junior didn't bother to answer. He just turned and headed toward the garage after the others.

Kin turned to go, too, wondering if Teresa would follow. She did, falling easily into step beside him.

"They're pretty bummed out," she said. "I guess they're worried about qualifying. They have to make it in the top twenty-five today, or else they'll have to try again tomorrow."

"I know," Kin said quickly. He didn't want Teresa to think he didn't know anything about racing. He also didn't want her to forget that he was part of this team, too, even if he hadn't done much so far today except stand around and watch. "Then we'd lose a lot of valuable time that could have been used to work on our race-day setup."

Teresa didn't answer for a moment, and they walked along in silence. Kin couldn't help noticing the way her long, slender legs swung forward as she strode beside him.

When they reached the garage, Cope was grumbling about the qualifying. "We'll be lucky to make it into the top twenty-five," he muttered, staring gloomily at his clipboard.

Tach nodded glumly, running one hand over his close-shorn gray hair. "Forget about pole position."

Waddy had already climbed out of the car and was wiping his face with a rag. Junior handed him a bottle of Gatorade, and Waddy took a long, hard drink before speaking.

"Well," he said at last, his voice heavy and bitter. "That was a barrel of laughs. I just hope our sponsor doesn't hear about it." The Peytona team had recently found a new sponsor, a guitar manufacturer named Hollis Wabash the Third.

Teresa hurried forward, looking worried. "Don't worry, Daddy," she said softly. "Things'll go better this afternoon. Don't beat yourself up, okay?"

Kin's heart ached. She looked more beautiful than ever with that caring, concerned look on her face.

"Thanks, darlin'," Waddy said, but his expression didn't soften much.

Teresa stepped back with a sigh. She glanced at Kin. "Want to go over to Infield Annie's with me and get something to eat?"

Kin did his best to smile nonchalantly, not wanting Teresa to see just how great that sounded to him—and not just because he was hungry. "Sure," he said. "I'm starved. Let's go."

"Not so fast, son," Waddy said without looking up from his Gatorade. "We've got work to do. We've got to figure out what changes to make— and make them—before qualifying. When the car is ready to go out, we can eat. All of us."

"But Daddy," Teresa protested, "it's lunchtime!"

Waddy smiled at her, though Kin thought it looked a bit forced. "I wasn't talking about you, honey bunch," he told his daughter. "You can eat anytime you want."

She shook her head. "It's you I'm worried about, Daddy. Sometimes you just try too hard. You'll make yourself sick."

Waddy's smile was a little wider this time. "You don't have to worry about me, darlin'. But I'll tell you what. Why don't you get a box out of the hauler there—I think there's a big old empty carton right by the door—and go over to Annie's. Get her to fill it up with mashed potatoes, beans, greens, whatever she's got. And some paper plates."

"And don't forget the corn bread," Carl put in.

"Right," Waddy agreed. "Get her to give you enough for nine people."

Kin glanced around the garage. Waddy, Cope, Carl, Tach, Junior, Teresa . . . "There are only seven of us," he corrected.

Waddy grinned. "I know. But Cope and I are pretty hungry."

"Okay, Daddy." Teresa leaned into the hauler to grab the box. "But you know that if I ask for enough for nine, Annie's likely to give me at least enough for ten."

"I got no problem with that," Waddy said. "I bet our new man Kin is pretty hungry, too."

Teresa smiled and hurried off. Kin watched her go, part of him wishing he could be going with her. But another part was happy to be right where he was, hard work or not. After all, Waddy had just called him his "new man."

OH, SAY CAN YOU SEE

During the slow hours after the breakfast rush ended, Laura had had plenty of time to think about Aunt Adrian and Uncle Smedley. A few customers wandered in and out, in search of coffee or sodas, but Annie's restaurant was nowhere near as busy as the morning hours had been. As she wiped down a table with a damp rag, Laura wondered if Laptop was still planning on digging up a million dollars with that metal detector.

Probably, she told herself with a grimace. *That kid doesn't give up easily.*

Just then Annie stepped out from behind the counter. "Heads up, Laura," she said. "It's about that time."

"Lunchtime?" Laura asked, glancing at her watch.

"End of morning practice time," Annie said. "Folks'll start pouring in here any second now, tired and hungry."

She was right. Moments later, the first wave of drivers, crew members, and fans started crowding into Annie's tent clamoring for lunch, and Annie and Laura had to get down to some serious work.

It was hot work, too, ladling beans and ham from a pot and pulling pans of corn bread from a hot oven. Laura pulled up her apron to wipe the sweat from her upper lip. No doubt about it—if she had a choice of careers, she'd take singer over race track cook any day.

A few minutes later Laptop showed up with Hotshoe and Scuffs. While her grandfather was finding a seat, Laura pulled her little brother aside. "Any brilliant new ideas?" she asked a bit sarcastically. She still hadn't quite forgiven him for blurting out their family problems to Jane and Eddie yesterday.

Laptop shook his head sadly. "I couldn't get away from Grandpa all morning," he reported. "I'm going to tell him I want to take a nap after lunch. Then I can sneak out and go over to Jane's family's camper. I'm sure she'll let me borrow the metal detector again."

Laura wasn't sure that was such a good idea.

Laptop tended to find trouble when he was on his own. But before she could say anything, Annie called her name. Laura hurried back to the counter. "Sorry, Annie," she said. "I was just talking to Laptop, and I—"

"Never mind that, hon," Annie interrupted. "I was just thinking maybe you could rest your feet a spell while you sing a tune or two. That's what half these people are probably here for anyway."

Laura laughed. She knew that people came from all around to sample Annie's famous Southern cooking. "I don't think so, Annie," she said. "But I'll sing if you want me to."

"Wait," a new voice broke in. It was Teresa Peytona. She was making her way toward them through the crowd of diners, lugging a big cardboard box. "Don't take that apron off yet."

"Hi, Teresa," Laura greeted the older girl. Once again she couldn't help noticing how pretty she was with her smooth skin, sparkling eyes, and bright blond ponytail. It was no wonder Kin was so gaga over her. *Not that he'll admit it*, she thought with a secret smile. Kin thought he was awfully cool, but Laura could usually read him pretty well, and his crush on Teresa wasn't exactly well hidden. "How's it going?"

"Hungry," Teresa replied with a laugh. "I've got a big order for you to fill. Family style for nine."

"Better make it for ten." Annie was already reaching for her ladle. "I know how Waddy and Cope and the boys like to eat."

"Why don't you make it eleven?" another voice put in. "I'm heading over to see Waddy right now. I've been driving all night and I'm as hungry as an ox."

Laura turned and smiled shyly at the new comer, a big man wearing a spotless white suit and fancy lizard-skin boots. "Hi, Mr. Wabash," she said. She'd just met Hollis Wabash the Third this week, but she already liked him. She couldn't help remembering all the nice things he had said about her performance back in Sudden Falls.

Teresa didn't look quite as happy to see Mr. Wabash. "Hi," she murmured quietly, the smile fading from her face.

Wabash noticed. "Something wrong, missy?" he asked kindly.

Teresa blushed. Laura wondered what was wrong with her. "Are you okay, Teresa?"

Teresa's violet eyes filled with tears. "I'm sorry," she said, taking a deep breath. "I wish I didn't have to be the one to tell you this, but Daddy taught me to always tell the truth, no matter what."

Annie paused in her work and raised an eye-brow. "Teresa . . ."

But Teresa was already continuing. "It's the car, Mr. Wabash. Number eighty-two, the car you invested your money in. I just came from the garage, and—and the guys said it's not running right." She gulped. "But they're working on it right now. They'll get it fixed!"

Wabash smiled and patted her on the shoulder. "I'm sure they will. Don't you worry, missy. A guitar has to be tuned before it'll play right, and I'm sure that's true of a race car, too."

Laura bit her lip, glancing from Mr. Wabash to Teresa. *You can tune a guitar just by twisting a few knobs*, she thought. *A race car's a lot more complicated.* But she didn't say anything.

Instead, she hurried around the counter to help Annie with Teresa's order. Before long they were putting cartons of beans and ham and big hunks of napkin-wrapped corn bread into the box Teresa had set on the counter.

Just as Laura was tucking a pile of extra nap-kins into the box, a man wearing a checkered-flag tie and a matching sport coat entered the tent and strode up to the counter.

"I'm Chet Flagg, but you can call me Checker," he said. "I own this race track." He glanced at Laura, then over at Teresa. "Is one of you the singer I've been hearing so much about?"

Laura blushed. She couldn't believe how fast news traveled around the track. "I guess I am."

"Hi, Checker," Annie said with a smile. "How you doing? And there's no doubt about it. She's the one you want—and is she ever good!"

"I can vouch for that," Wabash spoke up. "I'm Hollis Wabash the Third, of Wabash Guitars, so I know good music when I hear it. This young lady's the real deal."

Laura blushed even more. "Thanks, Mr. Wabash."

"Well, I'm glad you're here," Checkers said. "I just got a call a little while ago. Our guest celeb rity just came down with a bad case of laryngitis, so he won't be able to sing the national anthem on Sunday." He smiled at Laura. "I was hoping you'd agree to step in and take his place. How about it?"

Laura gasped. "Are you kidding?" she exclaimed as Teresa let out a whoop and Mr. Wabash chortled with glee. "I'd love to!"

HURRY UP AND WAIT

Kin's stomach was growling so loud it could have rivaled a revving race car. But no one was showing any signs of stopping to eat. Waddy's car was up on jack stands, hood open, tires off. It looked to Kin like a huge yellow and blue frog in a dentist's chair, with three dentists peering into its propped-open mouth, trying to figure out what to do.

Or maybe he was just getting delirious with hunger.

All he could do was lean against the work-bench and watch. There had been a lot of action for a while, with the crew scurrying around under Waddy's impatient supervision. But now all that was happening was talk, talk, talk. Waddy and Cope and Carl debated and argued and speculated

— — — — — — — — — — — — — — — —

about how to make the car faster, while Tach and Junior and Kin watched.

"Standard operating procedure in racing," Tach said, leaning against the workbench beside Kin and leisurely cleaning his fingernails with a screwdriver. "Hurry up and wait."

"Why aren't you over there arguing with them?" Kin asked Tach.

The burly mechanic shrugged. "Problem isn't in the engine," he said, glancing up from his nails.

Junior wasn't paying much attention to any of the others. He had produced a local newspaper from somewhere or other and flipped through it to a story about Sunday's race.

Kin wandered over and looked over his shoulder, wondering how he could stay so calm while his father and the other men were getting so worked up. "Aren't you a little worried about this?" he asked in a low tone, waving a hand to indicate the arguing men.

Junior glanced up and shrugged. "No big deal," he said. "Happens all the time. Believe me, these so-called discussions are going on in lots of teams right about now, even the ones that were fast in practice."

Tach heard him and nodded. "That's right," he

added. "Some people want to win the pole almost as much as they want to win the race. Cussin' and discussin' are just part of the game. Nothing personal."

When Kin looked around the garage area, he realized that Tach and Junior were right. From where he was standing, he could see several other teams involved in discussions just as intense as the one in the Peytona area.

Then something else caught his eye—a flash of honey-blond hair. "Here comes Teresa with our food," he said, almost as glad about the one as the other. He squinted at the taller figure striding along beside her. "Hey, and there's Mr. Wabash with her."

"Wabash?" Tach dropped his screwdriver on the bench and stood up straight.

Junior groaned. "That's all we need at a time like this—our new sponsor hanging around. I'd better warn Daddy." He hurried over to Waddy, Cope, and Carl.

While Kin watched, the three men's faces went through some remarkable transformations. First they looked surprised, then annoyed. But by the time Teresa and Wabash reached them, nobody looked angry or upset or worried at all. Everyone appeared to be jovial and in good spirits.

"Howdy there, team!" Wabash greeted them cheerfully. "Thought I'd stop by and see how it's going."

"Welcome, welcome." Waddy stepped forward to shake the sponsor's hand with a sunny smile on his broad face. "Make yourself at home. I hope you're joining us for dinner—nothing fancy, but you know Annie can't make a bad meal."

At the word *dinner*, Kin glanced at his watch in confusion. Despite what his hungry stomach was trying to tell him, it really wasn't all that late. Definitely not late enough for dinner . . .

Then he remembered. Down here in the South, a lot of people still called the midday meal "dinner" and the evening one "supper."

Meanwhile, Waddy and Junior were clearing the tools off of the workbench in the hauler. Teresa set the food down nearby.

"Hope you don't mind, Mr. Wabash," she said. "The bench there is the cleanest place around and the nearest thing there is to a table around here."

"Doesn't bother me a bit," Wabash said.

"Sorry to say we don't have any chairs, either," Waddy said. "If you like, I could send young Kin there around, see if he can borrow something . . . "

Wabash waved his hand. "Forget it," he said. "I

don't need any special treatment. I've got two legs—
I can stand just like the rest of you. Now, let's dig in!"

It was too crowded in the hauler for everyone
to stay there and eat, so once he'd loaded his paper
plate with a heaping serving of Annie's delicious
food, Kin stepped out of the truck and perched on
a toolbox outside. He was hoping Teresa would
follow him, but she was talking to her brother and
didn't glance his way.

Instead, Tach came out to join Kin. "How you liking your first day with us so far, Kin?" the mechanic
asked as he dipped his corn bread into his beans.

Kin swallowed a mouthful of greens before
answering. "It's great," he said. "I'm learning a lot.
I just hope I get to do something more to help
soon. I feel like I'm just sitting around most of the
time while the rest of you work."

Tach smiled. "Don't worry, son," he said. "You'll
have your share of work to do soon enough."

Kin was just sopping up the last drops of juice
from his plate with his last bite of corn bread when
Waddy hopped out of the hauler and hurried
toward them. When Wabash was out of sight, the
driver's worried expression returned.

"Tach," he said. "I need your help. In a minute,

come in and tell me it's getting late, and that you and Kin and Junior have to get to work taping up the car. Then ask Wabash if he wants to come watch what you're doing. I'm hoping he will. Cope and Carl and I need to talk. Understand?"

Tach nodded. "Understand, boss."

"Will I really get to help?" Kin whispered to Tach as Waddy hurried back toward the hauler.

"Sure," Tach said. "You'll get to handle a real roll of tape."

Soon Wabash was standing by the front end of the car, eating another helping of beans and corn bread. Teresa was standing next to him. Waddy, Cope, and Carl had disappeared. Kin suspected that they had gone off behind the hauler where they could argue without being heard, and he knew it was his job to help Tach and Junior keep Wabash distracted. Besides that, he was excited about finally getting his hands on the car.

"This is cool," he said as Junior tossed him a roll of tape.

Junior rolled his eyes. "Any dummy can tape." He grinned and cast a sly look in his sister's direction. "I mean, even Teresa helps with it sometimes, and if she can do it, anyone can."

Kin glanced at Teresa, expecting a quick, spir
ited response. But she didn't seem to have heard
Junior's comment. She was glancing over her
shoulder toward the hauler, looking upset.

I wonder what that's about, Kin thought. But he
didn't have time to worry about it at the moment. Mr.
Wabash was stepping forward to peer at the tape.

"What exactly do you do with that?" he asked,
as the two boys set to work, with Junior showing
Kin what to do.

"It's duct tape," Tach explained. "Around here
we call it two-hundred-mile-an-hour tape because
it'll hold a windshield or anything else in place at
that speed. Heck, with that stuff your Aunt Millie
could ride her motorcycle at two hundred miles an
hour and her wig wouldn't blow off."

Wabash chortled. "I think you're referring to my
great-aunt Gladys, actually."

Tach grinned and continued. "In qualifying,
speed is the main thing. Endurance comes later, in
the race itself. What the boys are doing is taping up
the grille so air won't flow through it. It'll make the
car slightly faster, more streamlined."

"Won't it overheat?" Wabash asked.

"Not in a couple of laps," Junior spoke up.

"That's all we need for qualifying."

Tach nodded. "We even replace the ordinary fan with a flat-bladed one. A flat-bladed fan doesn't try to pull any air through the engine compartment, so it takes a little less power from the motor. Every little bit adds up. Another thing we do to save power is disconnect the alternator. And then—"

"I hope old Tach's not talking your ear off," Waddy interrupted, coming up behind them. His face wore a large, pleasant grin.

"Not at all," Wabash replied. "It's fascinating."

"Well, I'm sorry to interrupt the lecture," Waddy said. "But I'm afraid we need to get the car set up for inspection and qualification in about an hour. Maybe Tach can finish up the lesson another time."

"Sure thing, Waddy," Tach said agreeably. "Talking's what I do best. Well, second-best, anyway."

Wabash laughed. "All right, then," he said, patting his ample belly. "Thanks for letting me hang around, Waddy. I'll be cheering you on this afternoon—and Sunday, of course."

Sunday, Kin thought. *The day of the race. But first we have to qualify . . .*

"Thanks, Mr. Wabash." Waddy was still smiling broadly. "See you later."

As soon as the sponsor was gone, things started happening smoothly and efficiently. It was a complete turnaround from a little while ago, before Mr. Wabash had arrived, when nobody had seemed to have any idea what to do next. Now Cope had a list of spring weights, tire pressures, tire sizes, and track bar and wedge-bolt settings. Everything he called for was done without question or comment. If Kin hadn't known better, he never would have guessed there'd ever been any difference of opinion in the garage at all.

Only one change generated any discussion at all. That was the rear-end gearing.

"Car seemed a little short on power coming off the turns," Waddy commented. "I think a lower gear might help."

Cope glanced at Tach. "Think the motor could stand two laps topping out at 8900 or 9000 rpm?"

Kin waited with interest to hear what Tach would say. He remembered that the high in practice had been 8700 rpm.

"Sure thing," Tach replied. "Stomp on it. Twist her tail off."

Waddy and Cope grinned. And that was that.

Everyone seemed relaxed and in a good mood.

Everyone, that is, except Teresa. She was still hanging around, but she didn't have much to say to anyone. Finally, when he had a free moment, Kin approached her, feeling a little shy.

"Hey, Teresa," he said. "Um . . . is anything wrong? I mean, I don't want to be nosy. But I couldn't help noticing . . . I mean . . . " He felt his face turning red as he struggled for the right thing to say. He didn't want to be a busybody, and he didn't want Teresa to think he was spending a lot of time watching her. But he couldn't help being concerned when the normally outgoing, talkative girl looked so glum.

"Oh, it's no big deal," she said with a sigh. She glanced over at her father, who was leaning in the car window. "Daddy's just a little ticked off at me right now, that's all."

"Why?"

Teresa bit her lip. "I told Mr. Wabash the car wasn't running right this morning." She shrugged. "Daddy didn't think I should have done that. He said just because something's the truth doesn't mean it always needs telling. But Mr. Wabash asked me, and I wouldn't feel right lying to him."

Kin thought about that. He could see both sides of the issue. Teresa had told the truth because she was an honest person, and that was good. But Waddy didn't want his new sponsor to worry that things weren't going well, especially since the car would probably be just fine by the time it hit the track for time trials.

He tried to think of something to make Teresa feel better. "I'm sure he won't stay mad for long," he said.

She shrugged and tilted her head to one side, setting her long ponytail swinging. "He never does," she agreed. "Daddy has a temper, but he never holds a grudge. He probably forgot about it already." She smiled gratefully at Kin. "Thanks, Kin."

"No problem." Kin's heart was singing as he walked over to rejoin the rest of the crew. The car was just about ready to go, and Junior, Tach, and Carl were starting to clean up.

As Kin hurried to help them, he passed Waddy and Cope, who were talking to each other in low tones.

"Waddy, with all these changes, I'm afraid you're going to get out there and this sucker's going to fall on its face," Cope said with a sigh.

Waddy shook his head. "I'm not worried about that," he said. "I'm worried about it being loose as a goose and sticking me and my rear end up against that concrete wall in turn four."

OFF THE WALL

A short time later that afternoon, forty-nine cars were prepared to attempt to qualify. Every owner or driver or crew chief who drew was hoping to pull out slip forty-nine, so his car would be the last one out, when the sun would be lowest, the track fastest.

Waddy wasn't one of the lucky ones that day. He drew number four.

Kin stood close to Cope when Waddy went out. He wanted to hear the time as soon as Cope had it. The rest of the crew huddled nearby for the same reason. Everyone wanted to hear the fateful number from the crew chief, even though it would be announced over the PA system. Teresa was standing with the group, too, close enough for Kin to smell the sweet, clean shampoo scent of her hair even over the stronger smells of the track.

Earlier that day Junior had explained to Kin that the Seabreeze Raceway was an oddball track. It had been designed and built as a one-mile track, and for a long time that's what Checker Flagg had claimed it was. But when Flagg obtained NASCAR sanctioning, NASCAR officials came in and measured it.

"They said it might be one mile," Junior had joked, "if the cars ran about three feet outside the fence."

Checker hadn't wanted to expand the track, and even though several drivers had joked that they were willing to drive outside the fence if that was what it took, the track stood as NASCAR had measured it. The official distance was 0.931 miles, which meant that the Seabreeze 250, with 250 laps, was 232.75 miles long.

That morning in practice, Waddy had been turning laps at 23.80 seconds, which was about 139 miles per hour. After watching a few of the other teams' practice runs, Kin had realized that lap times of 23-something were pretty standard.

He'd also been able to figure out the shorthand that Cope and Waddy and everyone else on pit road were using. A good lap of 23.70 was a "sev enty." A 23.67 was a "sixty-seven."

Up and down pit road, the talk was that Mark Martin had turned a fifty-five in practice and would probably win the pole. So when Waddy completed his first qualifying lap and Cope looked at his stopwatch and said "ninety-two," everyone on the team groaned, including Kin.

"Dang," Carl said softly. "And after all those changes we made!"

Cope blinked his large, pale-blue eyes. "Patience," he said. "Once the tires get warmed up, the second lap ought to go better."

"Yeah," Junior added hopefully. "It didn't sound like he had it quite twisted all the way that first lap."

Kin wished he could see what was happening on the backstretch. But the garages and the high hauler trucks behind them blocked the view from pit road. As the blue and yellow Taurus disappeared into turn one, all he and the others could do was look toward turn four.

They couldn't see Waddy's car, but they could hear it. "Hot doggies!" Tach exclaimed after a moment. "He's twisting her this time!"

By listening carefully, Kin could see what he meant. It sounded as though the car was winding to full power down the backstretch.

Soon enough the Taurus came into view once again. As soon as he saw it, Kin gasped. His heart began pounding double-time in his chest. The car was pointed down the front straight, but it was moving sideways toward the wall—fast!

"Oh, no!" Teresa cried, her hands flying to her face.

Kin couldn't make a sound. He just watched, frozen in horror.

The car drifted higher and higher toward the wall, while all the time the engine kept getting louder.

"He's not backing off!" Tach yelled.

A puff of dust went up, the car wobbled, brushed the wall, came off a little—and rocketed down the front straight.

Kin gasped in relief. "Yeeee-ha!" he cried with glee, unable to stop himself.

Teresa grinned and flung her arms around him impulsively. "He did it! Daddy did it!" she exclaimed. Before Kin quite understood what was happening, she had released him and turned to give Tach a hug.

Meanwhile, Cope slapped Carl on the back. "Sixty-three!" he crowed. "He turned a sixty-three!"

Moments later the Taurus coasted to a stop in

front of them and Waddy climbed out, grinning from ear to ear. "Well, we won't be anywhere near the pole tomorrow," he said breathlessly. "We may not even make it in the top twenty-five. But man, I'm telling you . . . " He looked from one crew member to another. "I'm telling you," he went on, "that was some kind of fun!"

Teresa rushed forward to give her father a bear hug. "Fun for you, maybe," she said rather accusingly. "What about us? You scared me to death on that last turn."

Cope grinned. "She's right, man," he agreed. "You about gave us all a heart attack. Why didn't you back off just a little?"

Waddy laughed. "You know the answer to that." He paused as the distant snarl of Jeremy Mayfield's Ford rose to a roar coming down the front straight. "After a while you get a feel for what a car's going to do. I knew it was going to get close, but all my experience told me that if I just hung on, it'd stay off the wall."

"And I guess it did," Tach commented with a chuckle.

Waddy glanced at him. "Yessir, Tach, old buddy. I just kept my foot on the floor and she kept diggin' and brought me down the straightaway. Straight. I bet if I'd lifted off, the rear end would have come around on me and I'd have hit the wall. What do you think, Carl?"

"Well, put it this way," Carl drawled. "I don't want you going back out there to try it again just to find out."

"Me neither," Cope agreed. "Okay, boys. That's enough jawing for now. Let's get this sucker back to the garage and changed to our race-day setup."

Kin started to follow the others toward the garage area. But he paused as Waddy glanced toward the track. "Just a second," Waddy said. "I just want to hear . . ." His voice trailed off as the sound of Mayfield's Ford faded into turn one.

"And there it is," a voice announced over the PA system. "A new pole-sitter, Jeremy Mayfield, with a time of twenty-three point six one . . ."

"See?" Waddy's triumphant grin had faded. "There's forty-four more cars left to qualify, and already we're down to second. If we don't stay in the top twenty-five, we'll have to qualify again tomorrow."

Cope shook his head. "Back off, Waddy."

"Yeah, Daddy," Teresa put in, taking her father's arm and pulling him along after the others. "You're nothing but an old worrywart."

EVERYTHING BUT THE RADIATOR CAP

As it happened, Waddy was right to worry. Even before the Peytona team was back in their garage space, Waddy was down to fourth place in the lineup.

Still, everyone was in good spirits as they prepared to make the changes from qualifying to race setup. Kin and Teresa had walked back to the garage together, and by the time they arrived, the car was already raised on jack stands. When he spotted the pair, Tach crooked a finger at them. "I could use some help."

"Just tell me what to do," Kin told the mechanic eagerly.

Tach grinned at his enthusiasm. "That's what I like to hear. Now, come on over here and help me change this engine." He glanced at Waddy's daughter. "You, too, Teresa. I know you've pitched in before, and you've got a good steady hand with the cables."

Teresa pretended to pout. "Me?" she complained. "But I might break a nail!"

Tach rolled his eyes while Kin grinned. He had known plenty of girls at his schools in Boston and California who wouldn't know the first thing about changing an engine—and who probably actually would worry about messing up their manicures. But Teresa wasn't like that. She came forward and stood beside him, waiting for Tach's orders.

"Okay." Tach rubbed his hands on the rag tucked in his pocket and surveyed the engine in front of him. "Now, I'm going to assume you've never changed an engine before, Kin. That right?"

"Right," Kin admitted, wishing it wasn't true.

"That's all right," Tach said agreeably. "I'll teach you. I'm getting tired of seeing you sitting up there on that bench relaxing while the rest of us work." He grinned at Kin. "I want you down here, by the front of this car, between me and that toolbox." He pointed to the large metal box nearby. "When I call for a tool, you hand it to me. When I hand it back, you wipe it clean before you put it back into the box, so next time somebody wants to use it, it'll be where it's supposed to be. And clean. Get it?"

"Got it." Kin glanced nervously at the toolbox. It was as tall as he was and had at least twenty drawers. How was he supposed to find the right tool in there?

Seeing his expression, Tach grinned again. "Don't worry," he said. "Teresa's right there to help you out. She's been handling these tools since other girls her age were playing with dolls."

For a moment Kin felt embarrassed. Here he was, supposedly an official member of Waddy's pit crew. And now that he finally had some real work to do, Teresa had to baby-sit him through every move. But he shrugged off the feeling. Everyone had to start somewhere. No matter what Tach said, Teresa hadn't been born knowing how to change an engine. Neither had Junior, or Waddy himself for that matter. They'd all had to learn from someone, just as Kin was about to learn from Tach and Teresa.

They began slowly. At first Teresa had to guide Kin at every step, opening drawers, pointing out tools, reminding him to wipe them clean after each use. But Kin was a fast learner. Before long he was doing most of it on his own.

Meanwhile, the entire crew kept one ear cocked for the announcements coming over the PA system. Waddy's place was dropping in the line-up—fifth, sixth, seventh—but not very quickly. When Waddy came over with Hollis Wabash in tow to see how they were doing with the engine, he seemed relaxed.

"Not too many good cars left to qualify, huh, Daddy?" Teresa commented.

Waddy patted his daughter on the cheek. "That's right, darlin'," he said. "We ought to end up in the top twelve, anyway."

Wabash bent to peer at Junior and Carl, who were both under the jacked-up car on creepers. "Looks like they're keeping pretty busy under there," he commented in his booming voice. "Changing a lot of stuff."

Waddy nodded. "We'll change the rear end to a higher gear so we won't wind the engine so tight. And we may stiffen the springs slightly, all the way around, because we'll be running with a full load of fuel, at least at the start."

Wabash glanced under the car again, then stood

to watch as Tach disconnected the last of the oil and water lines to the engine. When the engine was loose, Tach hooked a chain from the hoist to a lifting plate he had bolted onto the manifold.

"It's amazing, all the things that get changed," Wabash said.

"Oh, we'll use the same radiator cap," Tach said.

Wabash looked puzzled. "Radiator cap?"

Waddy laughed. "It's an old joke around NASCAR. You make so many changes after qualifying that you might as well jack up the radiator cap and run a whole new car in under it."

Wabash chuckled appreciatively. "Okay," he said. "Now, I can understand your changing the suspension and gearing and other things to their race setup before tomorrow's practice. But why are you changing the motor? I'd think you'd want to save it for the race and wait until after practice to change it."

Kin was glad the sponsor had asked. He'd been wondering the same thing himself.

"Good question," Waddy replied, rubbing his chin. "A lot of teams do exactly that. But I like to find out if there's going to be a problem with the engine. My experience has been that if an engine is going to blow, it's likely to blow early. So if this one's going to blow, I'd like to find out in practice rather than in the race. Also, I think we're pretty close to having the setup we want, so we won't be putting too many laps on it tomorrow. But the main reason . . . "

Carl slid out from under the car on his creeper. He stood up and brushed himself off. "Let me tell him, Waddy." He gave Wabash his slow, lazy grin. "You see, Mr. Wabash, there's going to be a dance tomorrow night. And so none of us want to have to work late after practice."

Kin's ears perked up at that. A dance? He hadn't heard about that until now. He couldn't believe Grandpa Hotshoe hadn't mentioned it.

At that moment Cope hurried toward them, clutching his clipboard. "Only one more car to go," he said. "Mark Martin's. Lucky guy. As if he wasn't fast enough already."

They all paused to listen to the next announcement. "Fifty-six," Teresa said with a low whistle, repeating what they had all just heard.

"That puts Mark on the pole and us eleventh," Cope said.

"But we're a close eleventh," Junior yelled from under the car.

Waddy nodded. "The whole top of the field is close."

Cope was shuffling through his notes. "Right," he agreed. "The spread from first to twentieth is only 142.26 to 141.36. That's just a shade over one mile an hour—only fifteen hundredths of a second per lap. Come Sunday, with the changes to race setups, we could easily be first."

"Or twentieth," Waddy put in.

Teresa rolled her eyes and leaned closer to Kin. "Daddy's always prepared for the worst," she whispered.

Kin returned her smile, taking a deep breath of the perfume of her hair and thinking of tomorrow night's dance. Would Teresa be there? Would she dance with him? Could he work up the guts to ask?

"Hey! Dreamer boy," Tach interrupted his thoughts. "Wake up. I already asked you three times to hand me that nine-sixteenths box end."

With a sheepish, mumbled apology, Kin did his best to push all thoughts of the dance out of his mind, and got back to work.

PLAYING THE PART

The rest of the afternoon passed quickly for Kin. Teresa wandered off to meet some friends after a while, but for once Kin hardly noticed her departure. After he and Tach had unbolted the engine and hoisted it out of the motor well, they used the hoist to roll the old engine out to the truck and bring the new one in and lower it into place.

Then Tach mopped his brow and glanced at Kin. "Okay, new man. Now I'm going to let you put in some bolts and attach a few hoses. But understand, I'll be checking everything you do. Not just because you're new to this. Even Carl and I check each other's work."

Kin nodded eagerly. "Thanks, Tach!" He set to work under Tach's careful eye, double-checking every bolt and every connection himself to make sure he'd done it right. It made the work go rather slowly, but Tach didn't seem to mind.

"Better once slow than twice fast," he commented a couple of times when Kin apologized for his slow pace.

Finally there was just an hour remaining until the garage area closed for the evening. Kin was wiping a few tools clean when Tach came over and put a hand on his shoulder.

"Carl and Junior have got all the suspension stuff done and the headers attached," the mech anic said. "They want to put the car on the ground. Why don't you help Junior get the tires on so we can all get out of here faster?"

"Sure." Kin stood up straight and stretched, noticing that his muscles were weary after his afternoon of work. It felt good.

By the time Kin and Junior had put the tires on and lowered the car to the ground, Tach and Carl had finished putting the rest of the tools away.

Cope checked his watch. "Lock that toolbox, boys, and let's get out of here. We'll have plenty of time to check things over in the morning."

"Yeah." Carl rolled his eyes. "If you or Waddy

don't have some vision in the night about how we ought to redo the suspension!"

Waddy came walking up through the garage area carrying a plain white box under his arm. "I just left Wabash at the garage gate," he reported. "Be sure you all stop and say hello if you see him on your way out. He's about the best thing that's happened to us all year."

"I guess that means we can go," Junior told Kin. He jerked his head toward the exit. "Come on, let's book."

"Right behind you," Kin said.

"Wait, Kin," Waddy said as the two boys started off. "Hold up a minute. I need to talk to you. The rest of you, hit the road."

Kin shot Junior a glance, but the other boy just shrugged. *What did I do now?* Kin wondered, fearing that Waddy was going to chew him out again like he had that morning.

He took a deep breath and followed Waddy into the cool canyon between the haulers. Waddy leaned against the side of one of the big trucks and gazed at Kin somberly.

"Okay, kid," he began. "Before I say anything else, I think I'd better show you what's in this box."

Kin glanced at the white box Waddy was holding, his brow crinkling in confusion. What was going on here?

Waddy pulled back the lid of the box. Kin gasped as he saw what was inside. It was a blue racing uniform trimmed in yellow. A name was embroidered on the left side of the chest—KIN TRAVIS.

"Nice, huh?" Waddy commented with a twinkle in his eyes. "Wabash bought new uniforms for the whole crew today. I thought you should be the first to see them."

Kin didn't know what to say. This was amazing. He was really part of the team!

"Hope the name's okay," Waddy said, poking at the patch. "Wasn't sure whether you'd prefer Kin or McKinley."

"Kin's fine," Kin managed to choke out. He stretched one hand toward the box, gently stroking the blue fabric. "It's beautiful."

Waddy laughed. "Isn't it though? This uniform is just for race day. There's another one in the box underneath, an ordinary blue cotton one for everyday. You'll put that one on tomorrow." He replaced the lid and handed the box to Kin. "Hope they fit."

"I'm sure they will, Mr. Peytona." Kin still felt a little breathless. "Thanks."

"You earned it," Waddy said with a wink. "Or you will, anyway. I'll see to that." His smile faded. "By the way, son, I hope you didn't take what I said to you this morning too hard. I know I came down on you, but it was for your own good, and the good of the team. It doesn't mean I don't still think you're a mighty fine kid." He shrugged. "But enough of that serious talk. Help me close up the hauler, and let's get out of here."

"Sure thing." Kin followed him toward the back of the hauler, the box feeling solid and weighty under his arm. But something else was on his mind—something he'd been wondering about all afternoon. "Can I ask you a question?"

"Why not?" Waddy started to close the big rear doors of the hauler. "Shoot."

"Last week, when we were at Pine Gap Raceway, you qualified on the pole," Kin said. "This week you qualified eleventh. But this week, you seem even happier about your position than you did last week."

Waddy chuckled softly. "Oh, I felt good about last week," he said. "But you see, the car was *right* last week, and maybe half the drivers here could've put it on the pole. But today ... well, when I came off four over there today, I knew I'd done the very best I could have. I mean, nobody in racing could have done any better. And I think that's what this game is all about—to know you've done the very best you can possibly do."

Kin nodded, pondering what the driver had just said. It made sense.

"Okay, we're done here," Waddy said, brushing off his hands. "Ready to go?"

"Um, you go ahead," Kin told him. "I've got to hit the rest room first."

Waddy nodded and strode away. Kin waited until he was out of sight, then turned and hurried through the silent and almost empty garage to the rest room marked DRIVERS AND CREW MEMBERS ONLY. There was something he wanted to do before he headed back to Grandpa's RV for supper. He felt a bit foolish, but he couldn't help himself. And he knew this might be his best chance for a while.

Inside the rest room, he set the box on a bench near the door and washed the oil and grime off his hands and arms. Then he sat down on the bench and quickly pulled off his jeans and T-shirt.

Opening the box, he pulled out the gorgeous blue and yellow uniform. Being careful not to let it touch the floor, he pulled it on and zipped it up.

He walked toward the mirror on the far wall and sucked in his breath. The uniform was a little baggy, but it looked fantastic! He twisted this way and that, trying to take it all in. The words PEYTONA RACING were embroidered across the back in big yellow letters. Just below that was a big patch that read WABASH GUITARS. On the front a huge yellow lightning bolt started on the left shoulder near the neck and came down across the front. High on the right side of the chest was another WABASH GUITARS patch. And on the left side, of course, was the name. *His* name.

There was one more thing he wanted to do. Stepping into his shoes, he stuffed his clothes into the box and left the rest room, walking with his head down in case anyone was around.

But he seemed to have this section of the garage to himself. He jogged through the garage, back to the area where Waddy's blue and yellow Taurus rested quietly, waiting for tomorrow's practice.

With a quick glance around to make sure he was still alone, Kin set the box containing his clothes on the car's roof. Then, trying to remember just how Waddy and the other drivers did it, he hiked up his right leg and tried to put his foot through the paneless window.

His foot didn't quite reach, and he almost fell. He reached up and grabbed a piece of the roll cage to steady himself. Then he tried again, managing to wriggle through the window and slide down into the driver's seat.

He was in! He grinned, liking the feel of it. He sat low in the car, almost as though he were sitting right on the floor. The thinly padded seat was stiff and unyielding, the padded-foam steering wheel thick under his hands. The gearshift knob was in easy reach, only inches from his right hand. The seat's side brace wrapped halfway around his rib cage under his right arm.

He took a deep breath, closing his eyes to savor the faint smells of oil and gasoline and rubber and stale sweat. He could almost see the track melting away in front of him . . . the long back straightaway of Talladega . . . the S-curves of Watkins Glen . . . the high banks of Daytona. He could almost hear the squeal of the tires and the roar of the engines. He could almost feel the air rushing past . . .

"Son," a voice broke into his fantasies.

Startled, Kin opened his eyes and glanced up. A middle-aged man was standing just outside the car window looking at him.

"Uh, wha—?" Kin stammered, embarrassed that someone had caught him.

"Garage is closing," the man said with a smile. "And Waddy, I'll be darned if you don't look younger every day."

DREAMS AND SCHEMES

"Kin looked pretty cool in his uniform, didn't he?" Laptop commented. "That lightning bolt made him look like Captain Marvel or someone."

Laura leaned back on the steps of Annie's Airstream and smiled, enjoying the feel of the cool evening breeze against her face. "He looked okay, I guess," she admitted. She glanced over at Grandpa Hotshoe's RV, which was connected to Annie's trailer by a striped awning. The five of them—Annie, Hotshoe, Laura, Kin, and Laptop—had sat beneath the awning a couple of hours earlier as the sun had set, enjoying a casual dinner of barbecued chicken and potatoes. They had been interrupted countless times by friends and neighbors stopping by to chat about the day's qualifying results, to

make plans for tomorrow night's dance, to specu-
late about Sunday's race, or just to say hello.

"Too bad Aunt Adrian wasn't here tonight,"
Laura mused. "She would have liked the barbecue."

"Uncle Smedley wouldn't have, though," Laptop
said. "I bet he hates eating with his fingers."

"Probably." Laura gave her brother a sidelong
glance. "By the way, you still haven't told me what
you were up to this afternoon." She had been busy
at Annie's place for a couple of hours after lunch,
and by the time she'd escaped, Laptop was nowhere
to be found. He had turned up at the trailer just in
time for dinner with a strangely triumphant expression on his face. What could it mean? Was it possible he'd actually found something? Laura doubted
it, but you never knew with Laptop. Unusual things
seemed to happen whenever he was around.

Laptop broke out in a grin. "Well, since you asked,"
he said, "I think Aunt Adrian's problems are solved."

"What do you mean?" Laura asked cautiously.

"I went back and borrowed the metal detector
again, like I planned," Laptop reported. "Jane and
Eddie came with me. We went out to that big field
behind the stands where not that many people are
camped out yet—"

"What?" Laura interrupted. "You mean you left the race track grounds? Grandpa would kill you if he knew that. Not to mention what Aunt Adrian would—"

"Do you want to hear what I found or not?"

Laura sighed. "Go ahead."

Laptop smiled and rubbed his hands together eagerly. "Actually, I'm not sure what it is yet. But it's something big. Huge. The metal detector just about went crazy."

Despite her skepticism, Laura felt her heart start to beat a little faster. She glanced around to make sure no one else was close enough to hear. "Really?" she said. "Did you dig it up?"

"We started to." Laptop frowned. "But then Jane's dad showed up and started yelling about us taking the metal detector without asking. He made us come in, and by then it was dinnertime anyway."

Laura leaned back against the steps again and thought about what her brother had just told her. Could there really be buried treasure out there? They weren't that far from the coast—anything was possible.

She shook her head. That was ridiculous. There was no such thing as buried treasure, not really.

She was just grasping at straws, hoping against hope to find a way to help Aunt Adrian.

"Jane and Eddie and I are going to try to dig tomorrow," Laptop announced. "You can come, too."

"Maybe I will," Laura said slowly. She still didn't believe Laptop had really found buried treasure—not really—but it sounded like he had actually found *something*. He might have a wild imagination, but Jane and Eddie had been there, too. And they seemed like normal people . . . Laura wished she could get Kin's opinion about this, but he had headed off to bed already, moaning and groaning about having to be up by 5:45 the next morning. Laura could tell he didn't really mind, though. She usually didn't pay that much attention to what her older brother did, but tonight she hadn't been able to help noticing that Kin seemed happier than he had in a long time—maybe even since before their parents died. She suspected he was sound asleep right now, probably dreaming of driving race cars someday, just like Grandpa Hotshoe once had.

Inside the RV, Kin wasn't asleep, though he was exhausted from his long day with the pit crew. His mind was racing, imagining everything that was to come tomorrow. First another day of practice, more of Waddy's three *L*'s. Kin had looked, listened, and learned so much already, but he knew it was only the beginning.

Then there was the dance tomorrow night. Kin's heart fluttered when he thought about that— would he finally have a chance to get to know Teresa better? Could dancing with her possibly be as fantastic as he imagined?

But that wasn't all he had to look forward to. The day after tomorrow, Sunday, was the day of the big race. Would the Peytona team's careful calculations and preparations be enough?

Kin shifted in his bunk and sighed. There was so much to think about, but he knew he'd better get some sleep if he didn't want to be too tired to enjoy it all when the time came. Finally he drifted off to sleep, slipping smoothly from his waking thoughts into dreams filled with the roar of engines and the smell of gasoline.

More later . . .